F
BY NIGHT

Hannah MacFarlane

© Hannah MacFarlane 2007
First published 2007
ISBN 978 1 84427 323 2

Scripture Union, 207–209 Queensway, Bletchley, Milton Keynes, MK2 2EB, United Kingdom
Email: info@scriptureunion.org.uk
Website: www.scriptureunion.org.uk

Scripture Union Australia, Locked Bag 2, Central Coast Business Centre, NSW 2252, Australia
Website: www.scriptureunion.org.au

Scripture Union USA, PO Box 987, Valley Forge, PA 19482
Website: www.scriptureunion.org

Scripture quotations taken from the New American Standard Bible®, © 1960, 1962, 1963, 1968, 1971, 1972, 1973, 1975, 1977, 1995 by The Lockman Foundation. Used by permission (www.Lockman.org).

British Library Cataloguing-in-Publication Data.
A catalogue record of this book is available from the British Library.

Printed in the UK by CPI Bookmarque, Croydon, CR0 4TD

Cover design by Go Ballistic Design Ltd
Internal design and layout by Alex Taylor
Internal illustrations by Helen Gale

Scripture Union is an international Christian charity working with churches in more than 130 countries, providing resources to bring the good news about Jesus Christ to children, young people and families and to encourage them to develop spiritually through the Bible and prayer.

As well as our network of volunteers, staff and associates who run holidays, church-based events and school Christian groups, we produce a wide range of publications and support those who use our resources through training programmes.

FOR ELIANA

PART ONE: EGYPT

1

"THE BLOOD SHALL BE A SIGN FOR YOU ON THE HOUSES WHERE YOU LIVE."

I should be asleep, but I am awake. Wide awake. And I am listening. Many unpleasant things have been happening here recently, and I'm certain something else is going to happen tonight. How do I know? Because Kiva was unusually quiet this evening. He's always quiet when there's something on his mind. He frowns and paces the room but, when I go to him and put my hand on his shoulder, he smiles at me and says, "Don't worry, Adalia, I'm fine. Everything is going to be all right." He doesn't like to tell me what's happening because he tries to protect me. He's worried that I'll be afraid.

I *am* afraid and that's why I'm still awake. I'm afraid to sleep because something's going to happen tonight. I know it. And that's why I'm listening. I don't know what I'm listening for. When I hear it, I will. But, for now, everything is silent. It's a still silence. A scary silence. It surrounds me and I'm afraid to move. Afraid even to breathe. I'm curled up under my blanket. My knees are pressing tightly against my chest. One hand is clutching the blanket, drawing it up to my chin to keep me warm. The rough wool itches a little, but it's *my* blanket and I always feel better when I'm holding it. I remember lying here – exactly like this – the first night Kiva and I knew we were alone.

I hear a movement. My eyes and ears become fully alert and I forget my thoughts. I quietly move one thumb to my mouth and nibble on the nail. *Is this it?* A halo of light appears on my wall. It begins near the doorway and the edges spread slowly, gradually, until there is a warm glow in the room. *No, it's only Kiva.* He's holding up the lamp to check on me. He's checking that I am asleep. That I'm not feeling afraid. I gently close my eyelids, feeling my soft lashes tickle my cheeks, and I breathe slowly, deeply. I breathe in, wait for a moment, and then breathe out. Breathe in again. Wait. Breathe out. In… and Kiva is gone. He thinks that I'm asleep.

As I wait for it to come – something that will tell me the trouble is here – I keep thinking about this evening, trying to make sense of what happened here tonight. Here, in our house. Everything so particular. Everything so carefully planned.

Four days ago, Kiva chose a lamb from among our flock. It's not a large flock, but the animals are our own and it's my job to look after them. I keep them clean. I feed them whenever we can afford to so that they're healthy. We sell the animals for extra money. I argued with Kiva, because I didn't want him to take the lamb he chose. It was a male, only one year old and absolutely perfect. I'm not exaggerating. He *was* perfect. I was so proud of him. He would have been worth a lot. I didn't want Kiva to kill him and I begged him, but he did it anyway. Tears stung my eyes but I didn't let them out. I didn't want to look silly in front of my brother.

This evening, Kiva killed the lamb at twilight and cooked it on the fire. I offered to remove the insides and boil the meat as usual, but Kiva didn't want my help. He wouldn't let me cook. The man from next door, Yarin, came with his wife to eat with us. They are old and have no animals of their own now. Kiva said that they would help us finish the meat. We ate in silence. I didn't know what to say to our neighbours. I felt ashamed that Kiva would not even allow them to remove their sandals. They didn't seem to mind, but I was embarrassed that my brother had suddenly become so rude. I looked to him for an explanation, but he turned away. At the end of the meal, my brother and Yarin took out the lamb's blood while his wife Jada and I cleared the table and wrapped up the spare meat. Later, my brother and I went outside to wave goodbye to our neighbours. As I turned back to the house, I saw the blood smeared above the door. My stomach lurched. I felt sick. It was on the doorposts too. It looked so horrible, so wrong. I wanted to ask so many questions – I wanted to talk about all these strange things – but Kiva threw me a warning look and I knew not to ask. I knew that it was all for a reason. That Kiva was doing what was best for us. I knew that I should trust him. But the questions haven't gone away.

As I came to bed tonight, I noticed Kiva take the leftover meat and burn it in the fire. Another mystery… He's usually so careful to make things last. I'm worn out from trying to work out what it all means. I am very tired now. I roll over to keep myself alert for a while longer. My eyelids are heavy. Listening to the silence has made me weary. I want to stay awake but I don't think I can fight sleep much longer.

2

"NONE OF YOU SHALL GO OUTSIDE THE DOOR OF HIS HOUSE UNTIL MORNING."

I don't want to die. I do *not* want to die. Please, Lord, don't let me die tonight.

Adalia is asleep. Thankfully. I've just looked into her room and she's breathing peacefully. Perhaps I should check again. No! I might wake her. It's best to let her sleep now. She'll be awake soon enough.

"Against any of the sons of Israel a dog will not even bark." That's what Pagiel reported to us. I will not die, then. I am Kiva. I belong to the family of the Ishvites, of the tribe of Asher, of the nation of Israel. I'm a son of Israel. I won't die tonight. I will *not* die.

Pagiel is a soldier; he's the leader of our tribe. He's a good man – trustworthy. I can believe what he has told me, so I have no reason to worry. But what if I forgot one of the instructions? Or did something wrong? I'm a *firstborn* son. No. I don't want to think about that horrible possibility. Don't think about it. Stop thinking and *do* something, Kiva. But I don't know what I *can* do now. There is nothing to do – except wait. My father would have known how to handle this. I don't. I wish I could ask him. I wish he were here now so that this awful responsibility wasn't mine. I know. I'll go and ask Yarin, our neighbour. Then I'll be certain. I'll be able to relax again. I'll go now, while Adalia sleeps. No! Pagiel said that I must not leave the house. We must stay indoors until morning. I can't go.

What now? If I die tonight, Adalia will be alone. She'll have nobody left in the world and I promised my father that I'd protect her. I *promised*. Perhaps I should wake her and explain, in case anything happens to me. Adalia tries to be strong but she can't leave here and travel alone. And we *are* leaving. After tonight there will be no choice. We won't be able to stay here in Goshen after this. I *must* leave with her. I must protect her as I promised. Adalia has never known a mother, she has lost a father; she *can't* lose a brother too.

How long have I been striding up and down this room? It must be nearly midnight. Please, Lord, don't let me die. I do *not* want to die tonight.

3

"THERE SHALL BE A GREAT CRY IN ALL THE LAND OF EGYPT, SUCH AS THERE HAS NOT BEEN BEFORE, AND SUCH AS SHALL NEVER BE AGAIN."

What is that?

I lurch forward so that I'm sitting bolt upright in my bed. My eyes spring open and do not blink, but they haven't adjusted to the darkness yet and I can't see a thing. I don't remember nodding off but I must have been asleep because the noise startled me. What is that noise? I'm awake now, but I'm not sure yet what's happening. I can't think clearly because of the noise in the distance. What is it? It's getting louder. I recognise the sound but I can't quite place it. What would make a noise like that? So loud. So painful. I cover my ears to make it stop.

Slowly I realise what is happening. I remember where I am. I had been waiting up for something. I tried to keep myself awake, but I was really full after the good meal. What is that noise though? It's worse than the drone when millions of gnats were swarming around the city. We had to shout to one another to be heard above it. Some people even used hand gestures but you could hardly see them through the thick cloud of insects. That was annoying, but this is much worse. It's worse than the terrifying claps of thunder and the crashing of colossal hailstones all over the land. Those made me hide under the table and refuse to come out, until Kiva laughed at me and called me a scaredy-sphinx. I put on a brave face after that, but I stayed near the table, just in case. People actually screamed in horror when the water of the Nile turned to blood – but even that was nowhere near as bad as this. These recent sounds plague my memory, but I know this sound will haunt me more than any of the others. It's a sickening wail. It's making my skin crawl, my stomach churn. And, worse than that – I recognise it.

I can feel the sharp pain in my chest like before. My heart is breaking all over again. I've not only heard this sound before. I have *made* it. This is the sound of pure grief. I know now that people are mourning. Hundreds of thousands of voices are crying out in anger and disbelief. It hurts my ears. They scream out their misery in unison. It shatters the stillness of the night. Maybe I'm imagining this. It's too horrible to be real. Maybe I'm having another nightmare.

I pull my blanket up to my chin and draw my knees up towards me. I sit like this for a while. I'm shivering, but I'm not cold. A minute passes; two, three and I just sit here. Listening. Waiting for this gruesome dream to pass. Remembering...

The tears roll silently down my face as the memories come back. I can see my father's face. He looked so weak, so frail, on the day he died. I felt empty that day. He was exhausted by the hard work, the years of service to the Egyptians. He worked extremely hard, but it was never hard enough for them. His work was excellent, but it was never good enough for them. It makes me so angry that he was treated that way. They would never let him rest. They didn't appreciate him at all. But he *never* complained. I miss my dad. I miss his warm, strong arms around me. I feel very alone here.

The noise outside continues to grow. It cuts across my thoughts, bringing me back to the present. I cannot be dreaming. This is much too real. Where is Kiva? Surely he has heard the chaos out there? He can't have slept through all this noise. Why hasn't he come to me? He usually comes.

"KIVA, KIVA!"

4

"THERE WAS NO HOME WHERE THERE WAS NOT SOMEONE DEAD."

 "Why couldn't it have been you?" barked Hakizimana's father as he dragged the sleeping boy from his bed by his ear. Hakizimana stumbled and fell hard onto the cold, polished floor. "Get up, you worthless boy", the voice ordered. "Get up!"

Hakizimana looked up at his father with fear and confusion in his eyes. His father was often angry lately. He had started shouting at the servants when his work as a magician at the palace had become more stressful: something to do with a couple of Israelites and a snake upstaging him. Hakizimana had found it quite amusing at first. He'd always known that his father's trickery was a fraud anyway. But, with each new challenge the Israelites made, his father had grown angrier. He had soon begun to take it out on his wife when he got home, then on Hakizimana.

Never on the older brother, though. Not even once. Hakizimana had always suspected that he was not only second in age but also second in his father's affections. While Hakizimana and his mother suffered daily humiliation, the firstborn just watched on with a smug expression in his eyes. Hakizimana had a strong feeling that

14

his brother was their father's favourite and now he knew it was true. He could do nothing to change that. But tonight was even more extreme than usual. Now Hakizimana was really scared. His father had never used his strength against him before.

"What's wrong, Father?" stammered Hakizimana as he struggled to his feet. He put his hand to his ear. It burned from being squeezed so hard.

"Why couldn't it have been you?" his father yelled again, louder this time. As Hakizimana tried to understand what was happening, he became distracted by the awful noise outside. His father hissed through his clenched teeth, "I asked you a question, child".

"I don't know."

"I beg your pardon?"

"I don't know, Father. I don't know what has happened. I was asleep. Please, I haven't done anything wrong."

His father grabbed Hakizimana tightly by the arm and marched him along the hallway. Hakizimana began to feel dizzy. The noise was overwhelming and nothing was making sense to him. He was shoved through a doorway. The large hand of his father held his chin firmly.

"Look," his father commanded and lifted Hakizimana's head. Slumped in a corner of the room was the body of his older brother. It was lifeless and limp. Hakizimana felt his own body begin to weaken. He lost his balance. For a couple of seconds everything went black.

His father's voice jolted him back to consciousness. "Your mother has gone", was all he managed to say before tears began to form in his eyes. Hakizimana reached out a hand to his father. He wanted to comfort him, and to be comforted. He couldn't understand what he was seeing or hearing. His father struck his hand away.

"Don't touch me", he said. "It should have been you."

Hakizimana did not know what to do next. He stood staring blankly at his father. He didn't recognise this man any more.

"The Israelites did this", his father spat out, "they say it is their God. Ha! You've got an Israelite friend, haven't you? That Kiva! You tried to keep it secret, but I've seen you talking together, making a fool of me. Look what his people have done to our family. Look! *Every* firstborn has died. Your brother, *my first son*, has been taken from me. Every firstborn among our cattle is dead and *even* those of our servants who were eldest in their families have gone. I have lost more than I can possibly replace. And my *wife*! My own *wife* has insulted me by... Where is she, boy? Where has she gone? Do you know? I DO NOT DESERVE THIS! How can I ever show my face in the palace again, after this?"

His narrow eyes locked onto Hakizimana and he lowered his voice. "I've lost everything and yet *you* survived. You who have chosen to mix with the people that insult us in this way! I wish that your brother had survived..." Then he finished with words that would haunt Hakizimana for the rest of his life:

"And that *you* had died."

Hakizimana ran from his home without stopping to gather any of his belongings. He did not look back.

5

"... GET OUT FROM AMONG MY PEOPLE ..."

 I'm glad of the chance to stretch my legs and get out in the air. I was only confined to the house for one night, but it seemed like the longest night of my life. It was really claustrophobic. Perhaps it was all the extra work that made me feel that way. Now that morning has arrived and I'm strolling with Hakizimana, enjoying the morning dew, that feeling has completely disappeared. *I am still alive!* That one simple fact makes me want to dance like an Egyptian! Maybe I'd dance right here in the street if my neck wasn't so stiff. Probably not though. I breathe in deeply. The air smells so fresh. It won't last long once the sun rises and heats everything up – then it'll be stifling. And the blood smeared around our doors will start to reek! It is quiet now too. Not many people are about this early. I want to make the most of this opportunity while I can.

I must have finally collapsed from exhaustion sometime after I checked on Adalia, and slept soundly for the rest of the night. I wasn't aware of a thing until Haki shook me ferociously this morning. I was pleased to see him, though surprised that he was there so early. He found me slumped over the table and said it was near impossible to wake me. He said he couldn't believe that I hadn't woken before. I wonder what he meant. He knows I always sleep in late and loves to tease me about it.

Haki is unusually quiet today and says he wants to show me something. He's probably plotting a trick to play on me. He'll trip me into the Nile, or kick a cloud of dust in my face, or act as though I've just picked his pocket so that other Egyptians will chase me down. Then he'll have a good laugh and challenge me to do better. He knows I can't win. An Israelite doesn't have the same status as an Egyptian here – if I pointed and called him a thief, they'd call me a liar and chase me down anyway. I don't mind though. He couldn't spoil my good mood this morning even if he tried. I am alive! *I'm alive!*

Before I left, I made sure that Adalia was OK. I know that she'd been a bit confused by the special preparations yesterday, so I made Haki wait while I looked into her room. She was sleeping late and I let her. If she'd been feeling anxious, she'd have woken me to chat about it. She always does. I'll explain it all to her when I get back. For now, I'm enjoying just being with my friend.

We turn a corner and I nudge Haki playfully with my shoulder. He doesn't react, so I do it again, a little harder this time. I'm expecting him to nudge me back. Perhaps he'll do it when an Egyptian is passing us, so that I bump into them and am forced to grovel my apology while Haki watches and laughs. I move to the other side of him, just in case this is his plan, and I nudge him a third time.

"Don't," he says. His voice seems sad. I look up from my feet where I've been focusing until now. I've learned that doing this helps me to be invisible to the crowds. I notice that his face is pale and tired. This isn't a trick. He genuinely means it. Something is wrong. I immediately stop playing the fool and follow quietly behind him. I'm waiting for him to give me some clue. He seems grateful that I am giving him space. I wait for a long time. He isn't yet ready to share with me.

We reach the very edge of Goshen and Haki stops. He doesn't say anything. He doesn't need to. He simply lets me look and take in the scene in the neighbouring region. Cattle corpses are littering the streets, already attracting flies. Egyptians are sitting in their doorways wailing or gathering in subdued groups to comfort one another. Suddenly, I understand Haki's mood. "Who died?" I ask.

"My elder brother," he replies.

"I'm so sorry."

"My father blames your nation. Everyone does. They're furious. The Pharaoh has ordered you all to leave." Haki pauses and I sense there is something else he wants to say. I wait for him to find the words. "I'm coming with you."

"But, your parents…"

"I'm coming with you," he repeats. It is a firm statement. A declaration. He has made his decision. There is no choice left for me to make. I'll ask questions later. For now I nod my head solemnly. There's a pause, underlining the moment. Then he breaks into a smile and playfully thumps me on the shoulder. I thump him back.

We turn away from the scenes of horror and begin to saunter back, making plans for the journey. We laugh and joke together again like normal until I hear somebody behind us calling Hakizimana's name. The smile vanishes from his face in an instant. His eyes widen in fear.

"It's my father," he whispers, his eyes fixed straight ahead. "Run!"

6

"THE SONS OF ISRAEL WENT UP IN MARTIAL ARRAY FROM THE LAND OF EGYPT ..."

 The main street in Goshen was broad, long and straight. The entire stretch was well trodden so the dusty ground felt compacted and solid underfoot. It was the major route connecting all the communities that were part of the families of Israel. You couldn't go anywhere in Goshen without travelling along at least one part of it. It was always bustling with people, so it was naturally also an important place for sharing all the news. Both genuine reports and outrageous gossip could be gathered there at any time of the day or night.

As the nation of Israel prepared for its departure, this same street had become as organised as the main kitchen at the Pharaoh's palace on feast night. The leaders of each tribe were clearing large sections in the centre of the street, meaning that anyone who wanted to travel along it had to stick closely to the edges and walk in single file. At intervals along its length standards were being raised. These were large, colourful portions of fabric raised high above the crowds on thick wooden poles. Each one was unique in its colour scheme and design, and identified the group that belonged to it.

Four of these standards were symbols of the four military groupings of Israel. They were the largest, most vibrant of all the banners and were erected first. The standard of Judah was positioned at one end of the street, and those of Reuben, Ephraim and Dan followed so that the whole length was divided into four equal sections.

Each of these military groups was made up of three tribes and each tribe also had its own standard. These were smaller than the military banners, though still extremely eye-catching. They were raised next, to divide the military groups along the street into 12 smaller sections. After the military standard of Judah came the tribal standards of Judah, Issachar and Zebulun. The tribes of Reuben, Simeon and Gad made up the military group of Reuben. Ephraim consisted of Ephraim, Manasseh and Benjamin, and the three tribes of Dan's military group were Dan, Asher and Napthali. The standards of these 12 tribes lined the street like the pillars of a great wall: firm and strong on their own, but far more imposing as part of the whole picture.

All the colourful fabric rippling in the breeze made it look as though a huge party was taking place. Everybody was much too busy to celebrate though. Some Israelites were plundering gold, silver and clothing from the Egyptians, some were gathering their sheep and cattle, and others were preparing dough, which they packed up with kneading bowls in cloth sacks to carry on their shoulders. Everyone was in a great hurry.

The first groups of people were already taking their places behind the standards of their tribes, each family raising their own small banner to identify themselves in the vast crowds. Everywhere people were rushing to take their places, clinging onto their relatives in an attempt to stick

together in the throng, battling with their frightened
animals to keep them from darting away.

After years of slavery, the nation of Israel was preparing
to leave Egypt.

7

"... SEND THEM OUT OF THE LAND IN HASTE ..."

I am trying to force myself out of bed. I've been awake for a while, but it's warm here and I still feel tired. I roll over and let myself get comfortable again. It's unusually quiet. Perhaps Kiva has slept in late too. Well, he deserves it. He was up very late last night. I think he must have been out checking on the animals when all the noise woke me up because he didn't hear me shout for him at all. I'll sleep a bit longer and then I'll make him a drink. He'll appreciate that.

Someone is knocking at the door. I rush to get there quickly so that Kiva isn't woken. It's Yarin and Jada, and they look concerned. "Where is your brother?" Yarin asks.

"He's sleeping," I reply.

"You must wake him immediately. We must all leave."

"But..."

"There is no time. The Lord has freed us from slavery! The tribes are gathering even now and we will leave this place today. You *must* wake him."

I run to my brother's room then stand frozen in the doorway, like a statue guarding the path to the valleys of the kings and queens. The blanket is neatly spread over his bed. It was not disturbed last night. Kiva is not there! A gasp escapes from my mouth and my eyes stare, wide and frightened. I sensed that something was going to happen. I heard the horrors of the night and I was so scared. But I was unharmed and I assumed that Kiva was safe too. I'm so stupid. I should have checked. I should have made certain that he was all right...

"Kiva is gone!" I stammer, confused and scared. "Last night, I heard the commotion. I called out to him, but he didn't reply. I think he was checking the animals. He's not been back. He didn't sleep here. I've got to find him."

I run to the door, but Jada takes me into her arms. She holds me against her chest and begins to stroke my hair. I pull away, but she catches my wrists and grips them so tightly that it hurts when I try to leave. She fixes my eyes with her steady gaze.

"Listen," Jada insists. I stop writhing for a moment. I want to look for my brother, but her voice is firm.

"If Kiva left the house last night as you say, then he was in danger." Yarin says softly, with sorrow in his voice.

"It's chaos out there. You'll never be able to find him!" interrupts Jada. She's still holding on to my wrists. "It will take too long and Israel will have left without you. Just imagine what the Egyptians might do to you!"

Yarin continues calmly as though she had not spoken. "He was the eldest?" I nod. "Then I'm afraid it is likely that he has not survived. The blood on your doorposts protected those *inside* your home. Your brother has been extremely foolish and you will certainly suffer for it."

"No!" I scream and yank one wrist free. With all my might I try to release the other. I've got to look for Kiva. I can't believe that he's gone. He wouldn't be so careless. He would *not* leave me.

"*If* your brother is alive," reasons Yarin, "he may have joined the crowds by now, already looking for you there. If your brother is dead, what benefit is there in staying here? The Lord has promised a better place for us."

I don't want to give up, but I'm afraid he's right. The same emptiness that I felt when my father died creeps over me again now. My brother is dead. If he was still alive, he would have come to me in the night. If he was alive now, he wouldn't have left me to sleep while our people left Egypt for ever.

It does not matter now if I stay or go. My brother is dead. I have nothing left worth living for.

I give in and stop fighting against Jada's grasp. She draws me to herself again, but I don't feel any comfort from her embrace. My heart is heavy.

"You will travel with us," Yarin assures me. "We will adopt you into our tribe and take good care of you. We must go now. We cannot delay any longer."

8
"GO, WORSHIP THE LORD."

We're squashed between a wall and the dead body of an overfed cow. Haki's elbow is digging into my chest and my leg is folded uncomfortably underneath me – it's beginning to go numb. We have "borrowed" a blanket that someone had used to cover a lifeless relative and we are using it as a sort of tent to hide us from view. The stench is disgusting. It's a combination of rotting animal flesh and our own sweat.

We ran hard through street after street in the blazing heat, ducking in and out of the crowds and dodging the wreckage of so many Egyptian lives until we finally lost Haki's father. He'd begun to tire and gradually fallen far enough behind us to be out of sight. We took the opportunity to make ourselves a hiding place and rest.

The fear of being discovered is still keeping us here. I don't know how long we will wait. Perhaps until darkness falls. We're afraid to talk in case somebody hears us, so all we can do is wait and listen. I can hear people swapping their stories of loss. Many are asking why this had to happen; some are blaming themselves, others are blaming Pharaoh. Almost everyone seems to be glad that the Israelites are leaving. They hope it will be an end to their suffering.

I think about Adalia. I hope that she's OK, but I know that she'll be worried by all the activity. She'll be wondering where I am. I hope that she'll wait in the house until I come. Then the three of us can go together. She's sensible. I know that she'll wait.

My thoughts are interrupted by footsteps close by. I feel Haki holding his breath. His body is tense. I want to let him know it'll be OK, but I don't dare to move either. The feet stop immediately beside us. I can see the sandals and ankles of two men. *Go away! Please don't find us.* But they don't go. Instead, they lean casually against the wall and begin to talk.

"I'm tempted to go with them," says the first voice.

"Are you mad?" the other replies. He seems totally aghast at the thought. "The Israelites have been nothing but trouble here. They've brought plagues upon us: they've slaughtered our cattle, plunged us into darkness and attacked our flesh with sores and boils! We're better off without them."

"We've caused *them* to suffer in Egypt for generations. We've oppressed *their* nation."

There's a pause before the second man laughs long and hard at this, but the first man carries on.

"Their God has power greater than that of our best magicians. I've seen their leaders, Moses and Aaron, in the courts and heard their requests. Their God brought these plagues so that Pharaoh would listen to him."

"Their God," the second man spits out the words, "has brought our people pain and torment."

"Their God has protected his people through it all *and* brought justice for them for the way they were treated here," the first replies. "I'm ashamed of my pharaoh and my land, and I am grateful that my life was spared."

"So what exactly do you plan to do?"

"I will go from here with them and worship their God."

With these words, the first man leaves his companion. I look at Haki in disbelief.

"It is true," he whispers. "Even my father is afraid of your God. He *has* protected you through all of this. Don't you understand? Your people are not leaving here because Pharaoh has driven you out. They are leaving because your God has freed you. He has better things planned for you than this."

I think about this for a while. I'd been terrified of the Egyptians, but now I feel unusually courageous.

"If that's true," I say loudly, "then we don't have to sit here and put up with this dreadful stink! We must trust my God to get us safely back so that we can leave this place together… you, me and Adalia."

I throw off the blanket and drag Hakizimana out of our hiding place. We are both laughing aloud at our own crazy behaviour, enjoying this new sense of freedom. Ignoring the stunned faces around us, we begin to run.

9

"... THE LORD BROUGHT THE SONS OF ISRAEL OUT OF THE LAND OF EGYPT ..."

"Ouch!"

Someone has just rammed into my back hard with their elbow. I must be bruised all over from being squashed and battered so much. I'm sandwiched tightly between Yarin and Jada and I can't see a thing. I'm not even as tall as the shoulders of most of the adults here.

Everyone is getting hot and irritable.

"Oh, my foot!" I hear a mumbled apology, although I can't tell where it came from.

Apart from concentrating hard on staying upright and intact, I am only vaguely aware of what is going on here. It's like a dream. I can see and hear things, but they seem far away and fuzzy. It's all happening round me, but I don't feel part of it. I don't feel *anything*. All I can think about is that Kiva isn't here with me. He never will be again.

I am surrounded by total strangers. I should be travelling with my own tribe, but I am secretly glad to be where nobody knows me. Some of the strangers stand on tiptoes and strain their necks to see over the heads in front of them. They chat excitedly, looking forward to what will happen next. Others seem nervous and cling to each other's arms, not knowing what to expect when we leave Goshen. It's extremely hot and many are just tired of standing. They wipe their foreheads and sigh, or shuffle their feet uncomfortably. Out of the hundreds and thousands of Israelites waiting together here, I must be the only one who feels nothing. I am numb.

From ahead of us comes the sound of movement, of many feet stepping out together. I watch the standard of Judah – my adopted tribe – rise up high above our heads, wobble slightly as the bearers take its weight, and then begin to progress along the street. A cheer erupts around me. The swell is triumphant. I hear it spreading through the crowds behind us, gradually disappearing into the distance. I take my first steps towards the Promised Land. This is a great occasion; history is being made. But I still feel absolutely nothing.

10

"THE EGYPTIANS CHASED AFTER THEM WITH ALL THE HORSES AND CHARIOTS OF PHARAOH ..."

"What now?" I call out to Haki, who has been expertly keeping up with every dodge and weave I've made and is still tailing close behind me.

"Keep going," he pants a little, "you can't stop now!"

I still can't believe the house was deserted when we arrived. I stopped dead in my tracks, not knowing what to do next, and Haki had to drag me out and force me to carry on searching. Since then we've run through street after abandoned street, amazed at how normal everything seemed, apart from the eerie lack of human life.

Now we're approaching the main street and I'm running out of both energy and inspiration. I round the corner without slowing and, for the second time this evening, stop dead in my tracks. Nothing. Not a sign. I allow myself a moment to catch my breath, then I ask the question that has been bothering me.

"Why didn't she wait for me?" I shout into the emptiness. My words echo strangely. Haki does not reply immediately. He waits until he's certain I really want to hear the answer.

"Many scary things have happened here. She's young. She can't have understood it all and must have thought you weren't coming back." I stare blankly at him, confused. He

31

makes it as clear as possible for me, not afraid to speak the truth.

"Kiva, Adalia must have thought that you were dead."

"*Why*?" I yell in anger. "I was always there for her. I protected her from everything."

"You weren't there today. Perhaps if you had explained these things to her..."

"Why didn't she wait?" I scream again. I'm angry with Hakizimana for being right. I'm angry with myself for leaving Adalia alone. I'm even angry with her for not staying in the house.

"We're wasting our time here, Haki insists. "Your sister is young but she's not stupid. She would have left with the others."

"What if she hasn't?"

"She *has*. There's no other explanation. And we can't stay here. Let's go, or we won't stand a chance of catching them."

Hakizimana has taken control of the situation again because he knows I can't think clearly. He's taking the lead now, running down the centre of the street towards the outskirts, and I've never been more grateful for his friendship.

"Come on!" he encourages and I speed up. As we reach the border, I'm amazed to see a large mass of swirling cloud in the distance. A long, black, winding shape emerges behind it, with tiny flecks of colour dotted along its length.

"The standards!" I exclaim. "It's Israel!"

Haki breaks into a smile.

"Then let's find your sister," he says.

We set off again with fresh enthusiasm now that our target is in sight. With so many people, they won't be moving fast. I'm certain that we will be able to reach Adalia quickly.

As we leave, I notice a commotion in the street behind us. Only moments ago, it had been dead and deserted. Now I can hear the hooves of horses clopping on the ground. It distracts me for a fraction of a second. I shake my head – I must be imagining things.

PART TWO: JOURNEY

11

"GOD LED THE PEOPLE AROUND BY THE WAY OF THE WILDERNESS ..."

 I have never been so tired. I have no idea how long we have been walking for any more. It is a long time – a really long time, I know that much. Days. Perhaps even more than a week. To begin with, I kept up with the pace quite well. A lot of people chatted to pass the time. Some even sang songs to give themselves a rhythm to march to. I didn't join in. I used the time to think. I was so lost in my daydream that I hardly noticed the walking. I thought a lot about the past few days.

None of it makes any sense to me. What happened to Kiva. And why? Can he really be dead? How did it happen? I have so many questions about Kiva's disappearance, but I know that I will never get answers. It doesn't stop me asking though.

After a while the singing stopped. Then the chattering began to fade. The constant footfall is the only sound now. People are getting tired. Their legs are beginning to ache. Carrying such heavy loads is making their shoulders and backs throb. Their eyelids are feeling heavy. I can't think so well now. It was better when the others were occupied. I could be invisible then. Now everything is quiet and people are noticing me. It makes me uncomfortable. We continue to walk without slowing. Instead of talking, people are beginning to give one another sympathetic glances. The looks in their eyes say, "I know exactly how you feel." They don't know how *I* feel. Nobody does. I concentrate on the ground, avoiding their gaze. I know that many of them are wondering who I am, what I am doing here. I just keep walking.

The awkward silence lasts until people can't cope with it any more. One or two individuals begin to murmur to themselves, quietly at first. Then muttering and complaining breaks out between groups until, eventually, everyone is involved and there is a full-blown rant about needing a rest. The tribe is irritable… All of them.

Everything the tribe of Judah do is done together. The people have gone through this entire series of moods as one. Just like they are walking as one. They are united. I am not part of this tribe though. It's obvious that I don't belong here. I am the odd one out in a unified tribe. I may even be the odd one out in the entire nation of Israel, and not just because I don't sing, or moan with the others. There's a far more important reason. What makes this nation keep walking together though this deserted wasteland is that they believe the same thing. Our leader, Moses, has told them that God is taking them to the Promised Land They really believe it. But I cannot.

All of the thinking I've been doing as we've been walking has brought me back to this one question: why has God taken away all the people I've ever loved? He let my mother die when I was born. He took my father away when I was still very young. And now Kiva too. Why am I left all alone? How can I rely on God for anything any more? I don't belong here with these people. I'm only here because I have nowhere else to go. I will have to rely on myself from now on.

12

"HE DID NOT TAKE AWAY THE PILLAR OF CLOUD BY DAY, NOR THE PILLAR OF FIRE BY NIGHT FROM BEFORE THE PEOPLE."

 The nation of Israel had been walking day and night. Since leaving Egypt, they'd camped only twice. The wilderness was inhospitable and harsh. For as far as the eye could see there was only a sort of yellowish brown haze; the colour of the dunes of sand, blown by the strong winds into sweeping peaks and troughs and covered with rippling patterns, like waves on the water. There were rocky patches too. Their colour accurately matched the sand so that they blended in, and they were totally bare. Occasionally there was a group of thistles, or a solitary acacia tree, but not often. In every direction the landscape was the same. Each view was just the same as the next. Because of this, it was very difficult to judge distance. Nobody was sure how far they had come, or how far was left to go. Travelling here was hard work. There was no path to follow. There were no guiding landmarks. At night the darkness covered the land in every direction with a deep and terrifying blackness. The wilderness was constantly and unbearably bleak.

In this bleakness there was one feature that stood out, immediately captivating and awe-inspiring. It was a focal point for the Israelites and they were following it closely. By day it took the form of a gently swirling mass of feathery cloud, hovering above and slightly in front of Israel. In the bright white mist, slivers of blue and grey were twisting and curling around one another in constant beautiful motion. It moved through the sky, as if in a breeze, gracefully enough for the tribes to keep pace with it. Its size and depth obscured the harsh light of the sun, making it possible to look ahead without squinting, and it provided shade, relieving the travellers of the sticky, oppressive heat of the day.

At night, when the pitch-dark conditions would have made it impossible to go on, the light, swirling wisps of cloud were replaced by the blazing roar of fiercely flickering tongues of flame. Bright flashes of orange and yellow light darted around each other, jumping and wrestling, twisting and writhing. The blaze of colour lit up the land for miles around, enabling the Israelites to continue safely through the harsh environment. The flames provided comforting and life-giving warmth, protecting the tribes against the perishing cold of the night.

Twice on this journey the misty wisps of cloud or flickering tongues of flame had stopped and come down to rest. Twice the Israelites had stopped too and set up camp in their tribes, moving on again only when the great pillar rose back into the air.

God was guiding the nation of Israel through the wilderness. The fire moved through the air, steadily, constantly, reassuringly, and the Israelites followed its lead.

But they were not the only ones following it.

13

"THEY ARE WANDERING AIMLESSLY IN THE LAND."

 This is much harder than I expected. We've been tracking Israel for days now. We started out running at full tempo, and then slowed to a jog. Now, though we run in short bursts, we are making slow progress across the tough terrain. We're taking turns to lead. One of us keeps an eye on the tribes and the other watches the ground for obstacles. I had not expected their progress to be so swift. We are travelling both day and night. In the day we seem to make up ground and gain slightly on Israel. At night, the challenge is much tougher. Though we have some light from their fire, it is really only a dim glow and our movement over the land is much slower. Frustratingly, we seem to lose any advantage we'd gained the previous day.

We had our first major breakthrough when the tribes set up camp. We took the opportunity to rest while the tribes organised themselves into orderly groups. It was awesome to watch from a distance. They were as busy as ants in a colony and seemed just as small. We each got a few hours' sleep while the other kept watch. Then, while the Israelites rested, waiting for the cloud to move on, we continued our trek. It was stiflingly hot and we were dehydrated, but we made a significant impact on the gap separating us from them. It felt fantastic.

Once or twice I've had the feeling that there is somebody watching us. Haki says I am crazy for thinking it out here in this wilderness but, although I can't particularly say why, I sense that we are not as alone as we think. Perhaps I'm imagining it. Maybe the heat and the exhaustion are making my mind play tricks on me.

Today we're making good progress. Haki is warning of obstacles underfoot while I make choices about the best route to take. We're jogging at the moment, and telling jokes to take our minds off the bleakness surrounding us. It's Haki's turn.

"Why are Egyptian children confused?" he asks, trying to keep a straight face.

"I don't know. Why *are* Egyptian children confused?" I reply in a singsong voice.

"Because their daddies are mummies!" he chuckles. I shake my head and deliberately don't laugh. I know I can do better.

"What did Moses' employees do when Pharaoh challenged him?"

"Hide!" whispers Haki. My smug smile fades.

"Yes, because they knew he would *strike his staff*. How did you know?"

"No! I mean it. Be quiet and hide", he hisses, grabbing me by the arm and throwing me down behind a large boulder. He hastily drops down beside me and peers around the rock.

"You were right", he says. "We are being followed."

I crawl closer to the edge and hold my breath. Two horses carrying Egyptians are cantering directly towards us. "Scouts!" Haki voices as softly as he can. "They work for Pharaoh."

We watch without moving a muscle as the scouts approach. My mind is racing. Why would they be following us?

Are we safe here? I know that Haki was determined to leave Egypt. His father was furious with him for some reason. Are they following us because of that? Had he committed some sort of crime there? The seconds feel like hours. I badly need to cough. It's dusty down here and my throat is tickling. My eyes are watering from holding it back so now I can only see a blur of movement where the horses are. They're getting closer, approaching fast. I mustn't cough. Too fast though. They're not slowing. They're not going to stop!

Then relief floods through my body... The Egyptian scouts haven't seen us. My cough explodes from the back of my throat. I pull myself up from the ground, dust myself off and I'm wiping my eyes with the back of my hand when they begin to slow and then grind to a halt after all. Instantly, I tense up again. They're only a little way ahead. One of them is looking around. I'm afraid they'll spot the rocks and search here. If they do, we'll certainly be discovered. They're talking to one another and one of them points into the distance. My eyes widen. They are tracking the Israelites!

Part of me is relieved at my own safety. The other part is even more concerned now. What do they want with the Israelites? They've only just released us. Haki and I watch them watching the tribes. We stay like this for a while, not daring to move on, not knowing what else to do. I look at Haki, wide-eyed; he is looking at me. We are thinking the same thing. We must do something. I can't think clearly. What can we do from here? There is nothing. Haki is poking my arm with one finger. He's gesturing to me to look. I follow his gaze and see that the tribes are turning dramatically. The cloud has shifted and they are heading back at a sharp angle; the trail of people behind looks just like the tip of a pyramid. Why have they turned now? Where are they going? The men on horseback have seen this too. They set off again immediately, circling around and heading back towards Egypt at a gallop.

"They will report back to Pharaoh", Haki emphasises his next words, "before morning."

"We have to warn my people!" I insist. I set off running before Haki has time to reply. I know he will follow. He does, without hesitation, and he's catching me fast.

"Stop!" he calls after me. He knows my impatience to reach them. "Just for a moment."

I stop reluctantly; we have a lot of ground to cover and not much time.

"They have turned," he reminds me. "If they keep to that direction, they'll be heading for the mountains over there. He points out an imposing grey rock face. We can cut straight across and pull alongside them there. It's a bit steep from here, but I think we can make it. It'll be quicker than following their route." As usual, he's right. "And it's our only chance of getting there before the Egyptians!" he adds. He's already running as he speaks.

14

"... THE WILDERNESS HAS SHUT THEM IN."

 I was right. We have turned. We've come all this way, only to turn around now. We're not going *exactly* back on ourselves, but it really would have been quicker to head for this rock face in the first place. God has led us round the long way. And for no good reason that I can see. I knew I couldn't trust him.

I have no choice now but to keep going with the crowds. I could never make it back to Goshen alone and, even if I did, there's nothing left there for me. I'll have to tag along until I find a better solution.

Yarin and Jada are worried about me. I can tell because they're keeping me company in shifts. Sometimes, when they are especially concerned, both of them walk with me, one stationed on either side like guards at the palace. When it is Jada's turn, she tries to get me to talk. She says it will be good for me to share how I'm feeling about Kiva and looks at me with a wrinkled forehead, trying to see what is deep inside me with her piercing eyes. I don't want to talk. She wouldn't understand anyway.

I liked to talk to Kiva because he didn't ever judge me, he just listened. He used to understand me perfectly. Sometimes I tell Jada a little bit about my thoughts because I hope it will stop her asking more questions. Usually then she takes over, telling me a story from her past or talking about how wonderful everything will be when we get to the Promised Land. I pretend to listen, but I am not really interested. I use the time to think instead, nodding now and then to keep her happy. I feel bad that I am deceiving her. She is trying to be a friend to me. I don't want to talk though. I want my brother back.

Today Jada is chatting with her other friends in the tribe. I can hear them laughing as they all talk over one another. It is Yarin's turn to walk with me. I prefer the time with Yarin. He doesn't ask me about my feelings. Mostly he simply walks beside me. When he does speak, it's usually to point out something along the way or to comment on something that is happening in the tribe. Today he's humming to himself, leaving me to my thoughts. He is a lot like Kiva in that way and I like him for that. I feel comfortable and relaxed around him. I even feel like talking a bit. I think I will surprise him by being the first to speak for once.

"Have the first of your tribe entered the canyon yet?" I ask.

If he is surprised by the question, he doesn't show it. His face wears the same calm, smiling eyes as always. He straightens himself up, craning his neck to see.

"I think they have," he replies.

The mountain is towering above us now. It seems greyer and even bleaker close up than it did from the distance. The rocks that make up its surface are jagged and ugly. It casts a grim shadow over us. There is a gap in the rock face here. It is the beginning of a pathway through the mountain, a sort of avenue between two enormous walls of stone. It is wide enough for 15 to 20 people to walk through side by side, but the mountain is so tall that it seems much narrower. This is where our journey is taking us next. I look up and shiver.

"Will you be all right going in there?" I tease Yarin. He smiles.

"I think so," he replies, joining in the joke. "You'll be there to keep me safe!"

15

"THE EGYPTIANS ... OVERTOOK THEM CAMPING BY THE SEA."

"Listen!"

Haki stands motionless for a moment and strains to hear the sound. He looks at me apologetically. "I still can't hear anything, Kiva."

"It's ahead of us; a rumble." I explain. He crouches low to the ground, painstakingly listening. He shakes his head. He wants to believe me, but he's too honest to lie.

"I really can't hear anything."

I'm confident that I can hear them now. The blend of sounds is distorted through the various twists and turns of the gorge, echoing off the walls and fading as it travels, but I know it's not wishful thinking – I'm sure we are getting closer.

We'd watched as the long, winding trail of Israelites gradually disappeared into the mountain. As we got closer, the fracture in the rock became more obvious and, before long, we were making our own way along the dim corridor in our hasty pursuit. The snaking path narrowed dramatically in some places, with the giant walls of rock pressing in on us. Thankfully it always widened out again. Sometimes we were plunged into shadow by large overhanging chunks of stone and once we even had to scramble over a small mound of fallen debris.

"The Egyptians will have to clear that if they want to get their chariots through here!" Haki gloated.

The trek through the mountain now seems as endless as the incessant wilderness did before. Our time out there already feels like a distant memory. It's been replaced with this never-ending maze-like nightmare.

We make plans as we hurry along, trying to cover as much ground as possible before our energy is exhausted. I decide that, when we finally arrive, we'll head straight to the tribe of Asher and locate Pagiel. We'll tell him about the Egyptian scouts. He'll know exactly what to do. Haki agrees that this has to be our first priority. He says he isn't sure what the Egyptians are planning, but he seems very worried. After Pagiel has been alerted to the danger, he'll take the necessary precautions and I can concentrate on finding Adalia. She'll be travelling with one of the other families there. Somebody will be able to point us in her direction. She'll be furious with me at first – she's probably been really worried about me. But she'll be so thrilled to see me again that she'll quickly forgive me. She's good like that. I can't wait to tell her about our adventure. And to hear her story: why *did* she leave without waiting for me? I'm so relieved that it's nearly over and we'll be together again. I'll soon have answers.

Ahead of us a thin beam of light is appearing between the high walls of the mountain. Are we nearing the end? I speed up and begin to wonder what we'll find when we emerge into the daylight. Haki interrupts my thoughts.

"I hear them!" he shouts in excitement. He slaps me on the back. "We've made it!"

I smile as the unmistakeable sound of human life reaches my ears. I hear tent posts being hammered into the ground and people busily organising one another. I hear babies crying and children playing. I'm convinced I can even smell the delicious scents of food cooking on a fire. With every step, the scene becomes clearer and my smile becomes wider. I punch Haki in celebration. We jump up and down in the air and shout about how fantastic we are to anyone who can hear us. What a team!

Another sound joins the hubbub. It's a low rumble, like the one I heard earlier. What is that sound? It doesn't seem to correspond with the others. It doesn't belong. Suddenly, I realise why. The noise isn't coming from the camp. It's coming from behind us!

"Pharaoh's army!" cries Haki. He has stopped jumping and is rooted to the spot in terror. "They're catching up already!"

It is my turn to drag Haki along. I grab his wrist, yanking him out of his daze, and set off again at full speed. Thankfully his legs respond and he starts to run too, though his face is pale and he's shaking. I'm determined to get us both to safety.

Haki stumbles. I manage to stop him from falling and push him ahead of me. I am shouting constant encouragement now. I need to keep him moving. We mustn't stop. I'm afraid that we might be too late, that I won't be able to warn Pagiel… That I won't see Adalia again.

We round a corner, hurdling over a large rut in the ground, and emerge into dazzling sunlight. It's blinding. I can't see a thing, but I can hear panic rising in the voices of the Israelites nearest the canyon. They've heard the deep rumbling too, and they know it's not good news.

As my eyes adjust gradually to the light and I survey the scene, I understand why they're so nervous. The nation of Israel is camping on a large, flat stretch of sand. Beyond the camp there's only water. Lots of water. To either side the beach is hemmed in by the mountain range. The only way out is the way we've just come: through the passage in the rock. And the Egyptian army is closing in fast.

16

"THE PILLAR OF CLOUD ... CAME BETWEEN THE CAMP OF EGYPT AND THE CAMP OF ISRAEL."

The sun is setting. It is beautiful. Much too beautiful considering the rumour that's spreading through the tribes of Israel. It is the end of the day, but it might be the end of our lives. If the rumour is true, we will never reach our new home. We will all die here. I am watching as the darkness falls over the water and I sigh slowly. All around I see the fear and regret on their faces as it dawns on them that the distant rumble is the sound of Egyptian chariots. The people feel betrayed. They have followed their God and he has led them to their deaths. The Egyptians are coming to slaughter us here.

Jada has gathered as many people as she can find. A large group of her friends are kneeling in the sand, praying aloud. They still hope for a way out. I see no way out for any of us now. I cannot pretend to have faith, not even for Yarin who has been so good to me. Just now I walked away from Jada's group without a word. She scrambled to her feet to stop me as I left, but Yarin put out a hand and drew her gently back down. He let me go. Now I am walking alone by the edge of the water. I have gone where it is quieter, away from the angry gangs of men and the whimpering huddles of women, away from the clamour and confusion and chaos. I am waiting for the only thing that can happen now to actually happen.

As I walk, I begin to feel as though I *am* being watched. I slowly turn and look over my shoulder. I am being watched. A pair of dark, wide eyes is looking up at me from the rounded face of a little girl, sitting all alone. She is only about 5 years old, and she looks scared. She scans my face, trying to decide if she can trust me, clutching a blanket and nervously twisting a strand of hair. I smile at her, but I can't help staring. She looks as lost and lonely as I felt when my father died, and is about the same age. I remember exactly how it felt.

"Are we going to die?" she says, her steady gaze asking for the truth. "I heard a man say that we are." I look back at the water, surprised by the child's directness and unsure of what to tell her.

"You are alone," I stall. "Where are your family?"

"I don't know," she says. "I lost them."

"When?" The girl does not answer. I don't think that she knows. "Was it here, on the beach?" She is shaking her head and looking down at her feet. Her lip is quivering, but she is trying to be brave.,

"I... I couldn't keep up." I realise I am still staring and force myself to stop. I sit down next to her.

"Can I share your blanket?" She nods. She has obviously decided that she can trust me. "I lost my brother too," I tell her. "You and me, we can stick together.... If you like." The little girl smiles and her eyes light up.

"Can we?" she asks. I nod solemnly and take her tiny hand in mine. She is cold. Her eyes are still flitting around, searching mine for the truth. "We're not going to die, are we?"

I hate myself for lying, but I can't break this little girl's heart. She is so fragile and I want to protect her from this nightmare. I don't want her to experience any more pain. I meet her eyes with a firm promise in my own and say the exact words that Jada had just told me: "No. We will not die. I'm sure God is going to save us."

I put my arm around the girl's slender shoulders and wish with all my heart and all my soul that those words were true. She rests her head against my arm and falls asleep, exhausted from her distress. I feel the immense weight of guilt for my lie and a new sense of responsibility for this young life. I wonder how long ago she was left behind. How long has she been walking alone amongst all these people? I can't leave this girl now, whatever happens.

As I hold her, trying to warm her limbs and willing us both out of this dreadful death trap, a strong wind builds up from the east. The swirling cloud rises slowly from its place at the edge of the water. It drifts over the heads of the crowd, who nudge one another and turn uneasily to watch its progress. Nobody is sure what this means. Surely, we can't be moving? There's nowhere left to go! Silence falls over the entire camp as the cloud settles again – directly in the opening to the mountain pathway! It seems to block us off from the Egyptian army like a stopper in a jar. My own words echo through my mind. Could there possibly be any truth in them?

We will not die. God is going to save us.

17

"THE LORD ... BROUGHT THE ARMY OF EGYPT INTO CONFUSION."

 I'm still standing here, staring at the enclosed expanse of sand and so many frightened faces. Any relief I felt about escaping the canyon has entirely evaporated now. I don't know what to do next. I think of searching for Pagiel, but where would I begin? I think of finding Adalia, but there is no time. I think of facing the Egyptians and I'm gripped by panic. I'm paralysed by my own fear. I can see only problem after problem, so I stand rooted to the spot.

"Lord, help your people," I shout into the darkening sky. It's the only thing I can think to do. Haki is standing beside me – just as still, just as alarmed. He endorses my prayer with a simple "Amen".

A violent east wind arrives out of nowhere and knocks me back against the rocky face of the mountain. Haki stumbles too. The brilliant light that met us when we emerged from the canyon is replaced with a thick fog. Sand is being whipped into the air and lashes against my cheeks and arms. It stings and burns my skin. Only a moment ago the water was calm. Now I'm squinting and have my hands in front of me to protect my eyes from the salty wet spray that's coming in sharp bursts. I can only see glimpses of what is happening. I feel like I'm engulfed in a cloud. I grab hold of Haki and stagger forwards, bending low to battle against the wind.

"Keep going," Haki calls, "I'm here."

"What?" I yell.

"I'm right next to you. Keep moving."

I bring one leg in front of the other again. The effort is enormous and we're not gaining much ground. The air is damp and swirls around my face and neck, whistling in my ears.

"I... can't... do this," I say.

"Get down," Haki says and pulls me to the ground. "Lower!"

We're crawling now, using all four limbs to propel us forwards and grabbing onto anything that will give us a handhold. The wind is still chaffing my skin, hurling sand at my face, but the eddying, moist air is thinner here, and I can see further ahead. Beyond the crowds, colossal waves are rising out of the sea. From ground level they seem higher than I can believe is possible. Huge walls of water dwarf the Israelites, who are beginning to gather in droves at the edge of the beach. The wind is slicing the water clean in two, carving a channel through the sea! That is what the people have gathered to see – another canyon has formed, not through the rock of the mountain, but straight through the spiralling waves! I turn to Haki, stunned. The walls of water are gradually being forced apart to reveal the seabed. The scene is so unnatural. Can it be real?

"Haki, look!"

"I know," he replies, still shouting to compete with the wind, "the ground is as dry as a bone!"

The scene transfixes both of us. More people are gathering to examine the phenomenon and some sort of argument seems to have broken out at the front of the crowd. The mass of water is being held in place only by the swift movement of air. Everything in my mind tells me it is utterly unsafe, and others seem to agree. They are pointing and shaking their heads and shouting angrily. Others seem to want to go through. My heart agrees. These people seem just as angry. They are pointing in our direction at the opening to the canyon, which is now obscured by cloud. I imagine they are talking about the Egyptians – about how a moment ago we had no way out and about the path that has appeared. They seem to believe it is God who has given us an escape route. Haki and I continue to inch forward on our stomachs like snakes, watching all the while.

"They're going in!" he calls in utter disbelief.

A horse whinnies loudly close behind us. Then another. The Egyptians are terrifyingly close. There's more whinnying and neighing. The sound of hooves scrapping the ground joins the cacophony. The animals seem spooked by the cloud. Soldiers are shouting at the horses, trying to regain control, urging them on. I can visualise the scene in my mind, piecing together the story from the sounds. Chariot wheels are swerving and colliding, their loads thrown against the walls. Some Egyptians fall, their bodies landing heavily on the ground. The horses seem to be galloping away from us, their steps echoing off the rock and fading away as men shout after them. The army is in chaos, but they're still dangerously close.

I grab Haki and the two of us fight our way forward, battling against the wind, and emerge from the cloud to see another tribal standard disappear into the watery corridor. The beach is almost clear now. Those that haven't already taken the plunge are streaming towards the new path. We join the end of one trail and follow the masses that are funnelling down to fit the gap. Haki and I are the last of the last, but the crowds offer us some welcome protection from the wind's onslaught.

The waves are looming ahead. Behind us, the silvery mist of the cloud is closing in, barricading Israel from the Egyptian army. With one last look over my shoulder at the hastily abandoned campground, I force my legs to carry me onto the seabed. I hope that Adalia has taken this step too. I pray that our tribe is still keeping her safe. I promise myself that I will find her soon.

My entire body aches now. I'm willing my feet to keep moving. My legs feel as though I'm wading through thick, sticky treacle. They seem unnaturally heavy and drag, slowing me down, making me stumble. I want to rest, but I can't. I must keep going. In my chest, my heart is pounding painfully. I can feel my pulse racing through my temples, "Don't stop, don't stop, don't stop…" I'm sure that each heartbeat is audible, but all that I can hear is the thundering roar of the water. It's so loud that it drowns out everything else. I hear no voices, no footsteps. Not even my thoughts manage to reach me coherently over the drone. The sound is all consuming. It's the rush of river rapids over rocky boulders, the crash of stormy waves on the shore, the howling of the winter wind – all mixed together in a weird, wild symphony and multiplied a thousand, thousand times. It's incessant. Unchanging. Unrelenting. Like the darkness.

It's unbelievably dark here. There's a faint glow from the moon that casts just enough light for me to pick out the shadows of the people ahead. I can see a few immediately in front of me. Their bodies are leaning forwards, straining towards their unseen goal. Beyond that I can only make out a dark mass. The crowd has merged into one giant shadowy figure in the darkness. To either side, the colossal walls of water swirl and surge. They stretch away into the murky distance, as far as I can see and probably further. Much, much further. I try not to think about how much further. Try to ignore the nagging feeling that those walls of water will give way soon.

18

"... THE SEA RETURNED TO ITS NORMAL STATE AT DAYBREAK ..."

"Thank you, Yarin," I say as he places the child down beside us on the shore, and I mean it. He has been carrying her in his arms while she slept all through the night.

"She's exhausted," he replies. "She must have had quite an ordeal before you found her to have slept through all the pandemonium of last night. I imagine she's a tough little one, much like you." He winks at me knowingly, but he looks exhausted too.

"I appreciate your help; I promised her we would stick together but I could never have managed to carry her through there."

"I know," he says, "I was pleased to help. And I'm here for you. Jada is too."

"Yes." I nod, looking at my feet. I know that I must thank Jada too. She has been very patient with me despite my rudeness. I am feeling ashamed of myself. I walk over to her.

"Jada. I am so sorry." She turns and looks at me.

"You've had a difficult time," she says. "I know that you were angry with God." I nod. "You didn't want to trust someone who allowed pain into your life."

"But I was wrong to blame you."

"Yes, you were. I accept your apology though. You have done a good thing, rescuing a child. And a brave thing. She will be quite a responsibility."

"Will you help me please, Jada? I want to look after her properly."

"God will help you. He cares for you both."

"Yes, I know that now."

She smiles.

"Then I will be pleased to give you any advice you need. But the decisions and the responsibility will be entirely yours."

She looks back at the delicate bundle. "Go to her now. She is waking."

I am sitting by the still water, stroking the child's hair and thinking about the privilege that I have been given. She stretches out and looks up at my face.

"What happened?" she asks, "Where are we?"

"You have been sleeping," I reply gently. "God saved us, just like I said he would. We have crossed the sea and all the Egyptians are gone. You are safe now."

The child accepts all of this new information readily.

"What's your name?" the girl asks, kneeling up so that her face is directly in front of mine.

"Adalia," I tell her. "It means 'God is my refuge'. What's yours?"

"Nataniella," she announces proudly with an enormous grin on her face.

"It's perfect. You *are* my gift from God."

"I like you," she says.

I laugh.

"I like you too, Nati."

19

"... WITH TIMBRELS AND WITH DANCING."

Celebrations were erupting throughout the 12 tribes of Israel as they prepared for the next stage of their journey. Everywhere there was singing and dancing. The faces that had been filled with fear throughout the night were now radiant with joy and relief. People recounted their stories to one another, giving personal accounts of the treacherous wind, their family's fatigue or the proximity of the Egyptians. They especially enjoyed sharing tales of the two colossal walls of water collapsing back down on themselves, sending huge waves radiating for miles, and obliterating the entire Egyptian army in one awe-inspiring moment. Some took great delight in pointing out the heap of bodies, rigid and lifeless, washed up on the shore. Others spent the time laughing and sharing with family and friends, grateful that they were still alive together. Laughter and song could be heard right the way through the nation, as Israel celebrated the great power and goodness of their God.

Each military group gradually reformed itself into organised tribal units. In the hastiness of the escape from the beach and the imposing darkness of the water, the standards had provided a valuable guide for individuals to locate themselves. The entire nation was able to leave swiftly and remain on track, because of the familiar guiding presence of the coloured fabric banners. Anyone who became separated from their relatives did not stray from their standard and felt the reassurance of the certainty that they would soon find them again. Now the glad reunions were taking place as, within each tribe, families were staking their standards for all to see and any stray members flocked home.

The nation of Israel forged forward again in the heat of the day, following the cloud and their standards exactly as they did before. The terrain here was strikingly similar to the wilderness where they first began their journey. The heat was just as oppressive and the air was just as dry. The landscape was indistinct and offered no remarkable features. Israel's celebrations were soon forgotten as its members tired of walking. The songs faded to grumbling; the dancing was replaced with the dragging of heels. Their enthusiasm was swallowed up by the monotony of the journey until the stories died away. The party was short-lived. The people wilted like plants without water.

20

"THEY WENT THREE DAYS IN THE WILDERNESS AND FOUND NO WATER."

"Excuse me. Coming through!"

"Sorry, can I get past? Sorry."

"Excuse… thanks."

Haki and I squeeze our way through the crowds. Now that we've come this far, I'm getting impatient to see my sister again. I'm surrounded by family units, encouraging one another, sharing their burdens and keeping one another's spirits up along the difficult trek. It makes me miss Adalia even more. She must be very close now. After elbowing my way through another cluster of surprised mothers, I turn around to check that Haki is still with me. *Baaa!* A scrawny looking sheep scrambles out of my way and unsettles the rest of the herd with its frightened bleating. They're scattering in all directions now, getting under people's feet and generally causing chaos.

"Sorry!" I call out to a burly and very annoyed man as I grab Haki's arm and push my way through the next few rows of people before he can stop me.

"Oi!" he yells after us, but we're too far ahead to be worried about him. We're making good progress through the masses. A group of older men is having a serious-sounding discussion just ahead of us. As I pass them, I can't resist teasing a little.

63

"Yes, it is true, I agree. But *how* will we ensure that the tribe receives the nourishment it so desperately needs?"

One man actually begins to offer an answer, before realising it was me that spoke. His eyes widen in surprise before he furrows his brow, looking very stern. The others in the group shake their heads.

"Kiva! What's got into you?" Haki demands as he drags me away to safety diagonally through a large herd of goats.

"I'm just in a good mood," I reply. "I feel much safer now that the chase is over and we're surrounded by people again – *and* we're going to find Adalia before the day is over!"

I'm so certain of that that I'm already celebrating.

"Just leave me out of your mischief," Haki snaps back. "We left the beach the day before yesterday. It's nearly evening now. My legs ache and I'm thirsty."

I don't reply. I don't see how it's possible for anyone to be in a bad mood when things are going so well, but Haki's not the only one. Lots of people are beginning to moan about the lack of water here.

"*And*," he adds with feeling, "unlike you, I *didn't* manage to sleep through the party so I'm tired. Plus you've managed to irritate just about everybody in the entire tribe of Naphtali!"

He's right. I've been carried away in my own excitement and I'm certainly not making any friends here.

"Look," I say, "We're nearly there. Naphtali's standard is almost directly above our heads, so there can't be many more people ahead of us. We'll soon be home in Asher. We'll find Adalia, and then we can slow right down and take it easy."

Haki shows no sign of being cheered up by this news. He still looks thoroughly fed up with me.

"I promise." Still nothing. "I couldn't have got this far without you, Haki. Please don't give up on me now."

"And what then?" he blurts out.

I think he's really upset. "You and Adalia will have each other again, and who will I have? Nobody. You won't be interested in me any more. Nobody's interested in me. You're only concerned about finding Adalia now. You just wanted me to help you get here. Adalia, *precious Adalia*, is all I hear about. You don't care about our friendship. I don't have anybody!"

Wow! I hadn't realised that Haki was *that* upset with me. He must be more tired than I thought. I try desperately to think of something to say. But what can I say that will help? He interrupts my efforts with news that sends me reeling.

"My father told me he wished I was dead."

"What! When?" My astonishment is plainly displayed on my face.

"Before we left Egypt. That's why I wanted to come. I couldn't have stayed there after hearing… those words."

"But I thought you just came because…" I remember how I'd wondered whether he'd committed some sort of crime and cringe at my own stupidity. "I don't even know what I thought. Haki, I'm so sorry I never asked. Are you alright?"

"My mother vanished after my brother died. My father wishes I was dead. He's the only family member I have left and he doesn't want me. Now you're going to find Adalia and I'll be alone."

"I hope I'll find her safe. I promised my father I'd protect her – I feel so guilty that I lost her in Goshen," I admit. "I need to make sure she's still alive."

"I understand. Maybe you should just go on without me," he mutters under his breath.

"What? No! You're part of my family now too. I'm not going to lose you as well." Haki shows a faint smile. "And anyway, after a couple of days Adalia and I won't be able to stand the sight of each other, and then I'm going to need you again," I joke.

He laughs a little.

"Well, I suppose I'd better come with you then."

"I could've left you in that canyon, you know…. if I hadn't wanted you." I thump his arm. He thumps back. I thump him again.

"You'd never have got that far without me," he teases.

"No," I reply earnestly. "I wouldn't. You're my best friend."

"Thanks, Kiva."

We elbow our way through the last row of travellers and sprint across the gap that separates Naphtali from Asher. Haki is slightly ahead of me.

"Adalia!" He calls out. "Adalia, where are you? It's Hakizimana. Kiva is here too. He's alive!"

21

"THEY COULD NOT DRINK THE WATERS OF MARAH FOR THEY WERE BITTER ..."

Three days ago I found it hard to believe how anybody could have allowed themselves to lose a sweet little girl like Nati. We passed the day becoming firm friends. We sang songs and played games, she ran circles around me and twirled and danced, we discussed the people that we saw around us, I taught her to count: one standard, two old people (Jada objected to that, but Yarin grinned), three tribes of Judah, four sheep and so on. By the end of the day my jaw ached from smiling so much — I haven't laughed so hard since before I left Goshen. Nati fell asleep riding on Yarin's back, her arms draped over his shoulders. She was peaceful.

Two days ago I watched the sun rise, looking forward to another fun-filled day ahead. We started out well, but Nati was getting tired of walking. I began to understand how difficult it can be to travel with a small child whose pace is slow at best, and who stops to examine every interesting pattern in nature. She pointed out ripples in the sand that reminded her of pretty ribbons, cracks in the rock like lightning in the sky, shapes in the distant mountain ranges — a horse, a pyramid, a sphinx — and she craned her neck back to soak up the rich blue of the cloudless sky, stopping in her tracks and causing those behind us to have to stop too. I love her sense of wonder, but at the same time I was trying hard to get her to hurry up. And then she became thirsty. I didn't want to get frustrated with her, but often I couldn't stop myself getting annoyed. I told her again and again that I had no water, but I'd find some for her as soon as I could. I hope I sounded calm by the seventh or eighth time I'd said it. I was very grateful when Jada took Nati's hand and invented a sort of marching game to encourage her along. I was glad of the break and of Yarin's encouragement.

"You're doing well," he said. "She's learning to trust and respect you."

"But she doesn't listen."

"She does," he assured me. "But she can't understand your urgency. She's young. Be patient with her, Adalia." I was doing my best, but I promised myself to try even harder.

Yesterday we were all tired and thirsty and my patience, despite my very best efforts, was short. I couldn't blame Nati for whinging though – I felt just as fed up, and half the tribe were complaining loudly. It would have been unfair to stop her from doing the same. For most of the day I held tightly onto her hand and said very little. Sometimes I carried her for short periods. She would cheer up then, but it exhausted me even more and I became gloomier than ever. I'd managed less than three days before getting worn down by Nati; her parents had managed much longer. It was really hard work looking after Nati. I didn't know it would be so difficult. Jada was right about the responsibility. Towards the evening Yarin let Nati ride on his shoulders so that she could see further ahead. This gave me a chance to really tell Jada how I felt. I think she was pleased. Before the sea crossing I wouldn't have done that, and I have to admit that I felt better for the chat now. I decided to do better than I had done so far. Last night I walked along with Nati, listening patiently to her chatter and allowing her to twiddle my fingers in hers.

Now we have set up camp and I am relieved that there is water nearby. I have promised Nati that we will go together and collect some after we've had a short rest. My own throat is dry and itchy too, but I need to sit down for a bit before we walk any further. She is being patient. She is lying with her head on my lap telling me all the details of what she had seen from her perch on Yarin's shoulders. I am half-listening, enjoying the rise and fall and the rhythms of her voice, but I'm not really aware of what she is telling me. I'm just relieved to be able to rest my sore legs.

Many other people have already been to the water. They are returning now in twos and threes. Some are hanging their heads in disappointment, some are clenching their fists in anger and some even cry with frustration. I look at Yarin. Something's not right. He gets up cautiously and goes over to a couple that are making their way back. Jada and I exchange worried glances. I don't want to scare little Nati though, so I am not saying anything yet. Neither is Jada. We just wait.

"It's bad news," Yarin reports. "The water here is undrinkable. Those that have tried say its taste is horribly sour. They had to spit it out on the ground, even though they were extremely thirsty."

Nati sits up, flings her arms around my neck and bursts into tears.

"You promised," she cries. I look to Yarin for help. He shakes his head apologetically. I look to Jada. She gestures that they will leave us for a while and they do.

Now what? How do I fix this? Nati is heartbroken. I promised her we would find water to drink, but I can't keep my promise. I take a deep breath. I can only think of one thing to do.

"Nati," I say, prising her arms from around my neck so that I can look at her. "Do you remember how you thought we were going to die?" She nods. Tears are still streaming down her face. I wipe them away with a finger and tuck her straggly hair behind her ears. "What happened?"

"We didn't die," she sniffs.

"Why, Nati?"

"Because God helped us." I am pleased that she understands. I sit with my arms around Nati, looking into her eyes. I hope she will trust me.

"I think that we should ask him to help us again now."

22
"... THE PEOPLE GRUMBLED ..."

I'm taking a small detour for Haki. I'm pleased that, after everything we've been through, we've finally caught up with my tribe. It feels so good to be home, surrounded by my own people again. I never thought it would be so difficult to get here. Maybe I wouldn't have even tried at all if I'd known what we would go through. I'm just so relieved that we've arrived at last. I'm bursting to find Pagiel and to be reunited with Adalia, but I've decided to do something nice for Haki first. He needs that.

I make my way between various groups of people who have set down their belongings and stretched out on the ground to recuperate for a while. I overheard someone mention that there's water nearby, so I'm taking Haki to it by the shortest route I can. He thinks that we're searching for my sister, so I keep up the pretence, scanning around, looking this way and that. If I do happen to stumble into her, that would be fantastic, but there are so many people here that I doubt we will. I'm actually planning to search out Pagiel afterwards. Everyone here knows him, so I can ask around and he'll be easy to locate somewhere near our standard. Maybe he'll have some idea of who Adalia is travelling with. That will give me a starting point. I take a sharp turn to follow someone who's carrying a jar. I'm beginning to spot more and more people streaming in the same direction, downhill.

Haki is so faithfully absorbed in his task, searching for Adalia, that he hasn't even noticed the direction we're heading. I poke him and point towards the water. His eyes widen and he tears down the hill, hurdling over people's property and knocking things over in his excitement. He bypasses most of the others who are bearing that way, searching out his own route to avoid getting held up by the queues. I reach the edge of the water after Haki. He's already kneeling down, cupping his hands beneath the surface and taking a long slow mouthful. His face is submerged. I smile, enjoying his satisfaction and sit down, preparing to join him for a refreshing drink. Haki sits up, his cheeks swollen full, droplets dripping from matted locks of hair. He closes his eyes and swallows deeply. He's making as much of this moment as possible. I laugh. I stoop forward to sip from the pool. My reflection is gazing thirstily back at me, but Haki claws painfully at my upper arm. He leaves a deep scratch on my skin. I look up at him. His eyes are crinkled in disgust and he sprays out the remaining water from his mouth. It cascades outwards and lands in a perfect semi circle on the water. Haki wipes his tongue with the back of his wrist, trying to get rid of the taste. My heart sinks. Perhaps I won't taste the water after all. Further along, others are having similar reactions to the flavour and many have turned back, their shoulders dropped forward in disappointment. I can't believe it.

I storm through the camp, kicking up dust as I go. Haki calls after me but I don't reply. I don't even stop to look around for Adalia. I just want to find Pagiel. As I thought, he's not difficult to find. Like every good military leader, he is at the head of his troops. Now that most people are stationary, I storm through them and reach him quickly. As I approach, I can see him trying to calm some fuming tribesmen by settling a debate for them. I don't bother to wait for him to finish. I'm direct with my words.

"Pagiel, where is Adalia?"

"Kiva!" He is clearly surprised to see me.

"Who is my sister travelling with?" I demand. I don't have the patience to fill in the details for him.

The men who had been so angry with each other moments ago have obviously decided that their disagreement is not that important after all; they have backed off and are watching the exchange together from a safe distance. Pagiel stares vacantly at me.

"Pagiel! Have you seen Adalia?" I repeat.

"I thought you had been left behind." He speaks slowly, putting great emphasis on his words. "Where have you been all this time?" Haki catches up just in time to put a calming hand on my shoulder.

"Where… is…" I begin again.

"He did get left behind," Haki explains on my behalf. "He was helping me to escape from my people. We have followed Israel all this way and have only recently arrived here. Kiva is concerned for his sister's safety. Please tell us where we can find Adalia." Pagiel looks from me to Hakizimana, and slowly back again. He breathes deeply and swallows hard. His expression remains empty. He finally manages to speak.

'"Kiva, I assumed that Adalia was still with you in Goshen. I have not seen or heard anything of her since I left there nearly a month ago." Haki steadies me as my knees begin to buckle.

"Kiva, I'm so sorry," Pagiel finishes, "Adalia is not here."

23
"… THE WATER BECAME SWEET …"

"Adalia!" Nati shouts to me from a little way off. She has been playing with some other children who are camping nearby while I sleep a little. Jada has been watching to make sure that Nati stayed close by. I let her know that I will watch Nati again now so that she too can rest.

"Adalia, come here!" Nati's voice is insistent.

"What is it, Nati?" I call back, reluctant to get up so soon. There is no reply, so I pull myself up, stretching my arms wide and yawning. I stroll down the slope until I can see her in the distance waiting for me. She beckons me to come. I can't help laughing at her, her impatient expression is very amusing. I continue on at a leisurely pace, but this is not enough for Nati, who is racing back up the hill towards me.

"Hurry up, Adalia. You're such a slow chariot!" Those are the exact words I said to her whenever I was trying to motivate her to move faster over the past few days. She is mimicking my voice too. I pretend to look cross and stop walking. Nati puts both of her tiny hands in the small of my back and pushes with all her might.

"Come on!" she urges. "I want you to see something." I can tell that she is excited, so I hold out my hand and let her lead me to her latest discovery. No doubt it's a new type of

74

lizard that she's uncovered from its hiding place beneath a rock. By now, it's probably scuttled away in search of more shade – I hope she is not too disappointed or we could be looking for it again all day. And if we don't find it, I will be extremely unpopular.

Suddenly Nati stops. She points eagerly towards the water's edge and hops up and down in anticipation. Is this what she wanted to show me? I look again and notice a few people gathered there, but I still don't understand what I am supposed to see. A family is sitting by the water, chatting together. They are enjoying each other's company. There is nothing unusual in the scene. Nati rolls her eyes and drags me onwards again.

"It worked, Adalia!" she explains as she draws me down to ground level and scoops up a handful of water. She thrusts it towards my face, sending most of the contents splashing down my front.

"Drink this!"

24
"THEY CAME TO ELIM ..."

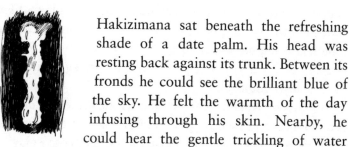 Hakizimana sat beneath the refreshing shade of a date palm. His head was resting back against its trunk. Between its fronds he could see the brilliant blue of the sky. He felt the warmth of the day infusing through his skin. Nearby, he could hear the gentle trickling of water dancing over rock. All around him people were soaking up the blissful atmosphere. Hakizimana wished that he too could relax and enjoy the delightful new surroundings. He knew it would do him good to rest and unwind. The journey had been gruelling and his body and mind were drained. He would really benefit from some respite. Thinking about it frustrated him. He looked at Kiva and sighed.

Next to Hakizimana, Kiva was sleeping. Since the dreadful distress of hearing Pagiel's news, Hakizimana had not heard a single word about Adalia pass Kiva's lips. He'd hardly heard anything pass Kiva's lips for that matter. By day Kiva stared beyond the horizon with a glazed expression in his eyes. At night he had slept fitfully, tossing and turning while his eyes darted left and right beneath his flickering eyelids, and muttering the same phrase repeatedly: "Sorry Father, I'm so sorry". Hakizimana was hopeful that the time here would help to heal Kiva. *He does appear to be peaceful for now*, Haki thought gratefully.

Hakizimana still couldn't relax though. He was worried. *Where was Adalia? Did she wait in Goshen after all? Have I brought my friend all this way for nothing?*

Something inside him told him that that wasn't true, but he couldn't pinpoint why he felt that way. It was just a vague feeling that he had. He had been so sure they would find her here. Hakizimana was feeling helpless to solve Kiva's problem and now he was extremely concerned about Adalia as well.

On the other side of the camp, Nati was worried about Adalia too. Adalia sat beneath the refreshing shade of a date palm. Like Hakizimana, her head was resting back against its trunk. She didn't hear Nati telling Yarin that she was concerned for Adalia. She didn't realise that Jada was speaking to her, offering her a drink. She was daydreaming again. Her mind was far away, preoccupied with other thoughts. Adalia had been daydreaming a lot lately and Nati thought that she seemed sad.

25

"THERE WERE TWELVE SPRINGS OF WATER AND SEVENTY DATE PALMS ..."

I sit with my feet dangling in the warm spring water. I rest my weight back on my hands and look up at the clear sky. Nati is playing with my hair as it hangs down my back. She is kneeling behind me, running her fingers through the long strands, twisting it first over one shoulder, then the other, plaiting it, letting it fall loose, then plaiting it again. A cluster of dates sits beside us on the ground and occasionally one of us will reach out and pluck one off the branch to enjoy its sweetness. I take one now and swirl it around in my mouth with my tongue. I look around again at all the trees. It is breathtaking here. It took me totally by surprise when we first arrived – I hadn't expected to find a place so beautiful in the middle of the desert. I'm glad that we are camping here for a while. It's good to enjoy the atmosphere and the chance to rest my body. That part of me – my body – is able to rest.

Unfortunately, there is another part of me that I don't think will ever be able to rest again: my mind. Though I am trying to appear relaxed, my head is full of thoughts about Nati's family and about Kiva. I can't help thinking that there is something missing from this blissful scene. If Kiva was here, then it would be complete and I could truly relax and have fun. But he's not here. He is dead. I also know that Nati's parents must be feeling the same empty space without her too. Do they think that she is dead?

"Adalia, why are you sad?" Nati asks bluntly. Maybe my act wasn't as good as I had hoped.

"I wish that my brother was here to enjoy this place with us," I reply, deliberately leaving out the part about her family. I talked to her about them once, soon after I found her on the beach and promised to take care of her. But she couldn't even tell me what they looked like. She also had no idea where we might find them. She couldn't remember the name of her tribe, what the standard had looked like, or even its colour. I had to stop asking questions because it was upsetting her so much, and I have never found the courage to raise the subject again since. I had no way of tracing them to return her. Now I wouldn't even want to. I would miss her too much. But I know they must miss her too and that makes me feel guilty. Nati belongs to her family, not to me. Even though there is nothing I can do to help reunite them, and even though without me she would never have survived at all, I feel awful that they have to suffer her loss.

"Don't be sad," Nati urges. She has moved to sit beside me. I look into her eyes and see the total innocence and sincerity of her heart. Nati simply wants me to be happy. For a fleeting moment, it occurs to me that, if Nati's parents think that she's dead, but she is not – she's here with me alive and well, then maybe Kiva too is alive and somewhere, even though I believe he's dead. It's a nice thought, but I dismiss it from my mind immediately. *It can't be true.* I will be disappointed again if I let myself believe it. If I knew what had happened to him back in Egypt though, it might help me to finally let go of this sadness.

As I drift out of my thoughts and back to reality, I notice that Nati has slipped away. I look round. Yarin is strolling towards me.

"Nati thinks I might be able to cure your sadness," he says smiling.

"You might," I say as I push myself up onto my feet. "But I doubt it."

"You underestimate me," Yarin jokes, pretending to be deeply offended. He puts on a scowl and turns away. It works. I can't help but laugh at his show of dented pride. I offer him the partly eaten bunch of dates. We walk along beside the water together a little way. Yarin doesn't ask what is wrong, he simply waits for me to tell him. He knows I will and, after a short silence, I do.

"Everyone here simply accepts that God is good because he has brought us to this place. Only a few days ago they were all complaining about him because we were at Marah where the water was undrinkable." Yarin's reply is short, but it gets straight to the root of my problem.

"People are fickle."

"Yarin, I *want* to believe that God is good. I know that he has done good things for me. But, if he is good, why am I all alone? And what about Nati's family? They must miss her."

"Yes, they must. God has not left Nataniella alone though – she has you and she has been kept safe." I look up at Yarin and he continues: "You are not alone either, Adalia. We cannot replace Kiva, but we are here for you."

"I know all that, Yarin." I pause, uncertain of how honest I should be. "But I feel like the only reason God has helped me all this time is…"

"Go on, Adalia".

"…is so that he can make me lonely. If he really cared, then Kiva would be here. It hurts to be without him and I can't stop thinking about what might have happened to him. A good God wouldn't put me through all this, would he Yarin?"

Yarin furrows his brow and looks at the ground. He is thinking about what to say to me. I know it will be wise advice, but I don't want to hear it yet. I carry on talking.

"I've tried to forgive him for taking Kiva from me, but I can't seem to do it. I'm not sure that I even want to trust a God who hurts me on purpose." I shock myself by speaking these words aloud, but they do not trouble Yarin.

"Adalia, I think that God has entrusted you with Nataniella because of these feelings you have. She needs someone to care for her who understands her loss. You understand her situation perfectly because you know what it is like, and so you are helping her every day in the things that you say and do. You are like a sister to her. If you did not have the experience of losing your family, you would not be able to help her through these tough times. And Nataniella is a blessing to you. I have seen you laughing together and it is good. There is pain. I don't deny that. Such things are hard, especially when we do not understand. But there is blessing too – if you choose to accept it. Accept the good things you have, Adalia, and enjoy them. You once told me that Nataniella was your gift from God. Do you still believe that?" I nod. Nati has become my whole world. I would do anything for her. "Would a God of torture give you such a priceless gift?" Yarin looks deep into my eyes before walking away, leaving me by the water, with his question fresh in my mind.

26
"... THEY CAMPED THERE BESIDE THE WATERS."

 My feet dangle into the water as it babbles past. Its movement tickles my feet a little. I rest my elbows on my knees and stare at my reflection in the clear stream. Haki is sitting cross-legged beside me. Every few minutes he shifts his weight to get more comfortable or puffs out his cheeks and allows air to escape loudly from between his lips. He keeps looking at me like he wants to say something. It irritates me. I want to be alone. I can't tell him that though. I shift my gaze towards the source of the water, away from Haki. He sits stubbornly, refusing to be put off from what he has to say to me.

"Kiva. I know you won't want to hear—"

"Then don't say it," I interrupt. Haki battles on anyway.

"I have a theory about Adalia."

"Adalia is gone. I've lost her. There's no point talking—"

"She's in your nightmares," he insists. "You can't just pretend that she doesn't exist and give up now."

"Why not?" I am being deliberately awkward and Haki knows it, but I do *not* want to be having this conversation. Like the excellent friend he is, he doesn't give up that easily.

"Because, Kiva, you'll never stop wondering what happened to her. The nightmares won't stop."

"Haki. I know you mean well, but I've looked for Adalia for a whole month now and I haven't been able to find her. I've done my best. I'm tired. I am not going to find her now. Maybe she doesn't even want to be found. Maybe she never even left Goshen."

"I think she did." He pauses to make sure I am listening. "But not with Asher."

"Maybe she got lost somewhere along the way. Or died. We don't know. We can't know. You're just guessing, Haki."

"Let's assume Adalia thought you were dead. She would not have wanted to travel alone. Who would she have trusted? Who would she have gone with?"

"Haki! Stop! I'm tired. I'm not going to exhaust myself searching for her any more! It's pointless." Haki is stunned. I knew he would be. That's why I hadn't wanted to talk about it. I knew that he couldn't understand. I feel sorry for him. I know that he is trying to help me, but he doesn't seem to realise how much I suffer every time I fill with hope and then deflate in disappointment. It's better not to let myself hope any more. I quieten my voice and try to appease him.

"Let's just sit here with our feet in the water and relax. Let's take each day as it comes. Let's enjoy life like we used to, be spontaneous and have fun." Haki does not respond. "Please don't ever talk to me about Adalia again. She is gone now…. For ever."

27

"... THE SONS OF ISRAEL GRUMBLED ..."

"We want to eat!
"We want to eat!"

Many voices were chanting in unison. There was an unofficial protest being organised by some of the more fiery-tempered members of Judah and the Israelite leaders were looking concerned. The oasis of Elim had been left far behind and was almost forgotten, and the supplies gathered so hastily in Egypt six weeks ago had entirely run out now. Many had lost patience and were no longer satisfied with quietly grumbling to one another. They wanted action. They were demanding action. One of the more influential characters called out above the chanting, "You have brought us out into this wilderness to kill this whole assembly with hunger!" A loud cheer of agreement erupted from the gathering crowds. Other tribes staged similar demonstrations. They were competing to be heard. The result was a cacophony of angry noise. It became almost impossible to pick out what was being said. A large number of the usually quiet mumblers were finding the courage to join in too, inspired by the confidence of others. They felt secure hidden in the crowd.

Yarin and Jada were standing a little way off. They watched the scene. Neither of them was afraid to be individual and different from the rest, or to form their own opinions, and so they didn't join in. Jada did not believe that such a noisy protest could be an effective way to put any point across – she would not shout as a matter of principle – but she was still very concerned about the lack of food. Yarin was reassuring her, standing close with a hand on her shoulder and speaking softly. He knew he was right when he told Adalia that people were fickle. He also knew that the pendulum of emotion would soon swing back the other way and the same crowds would be celebrating God's provision again. His years of observing others had taught him this. He thought to himself again how predictable humans were and shook his head, raising his eyebrows at the scene.

It was getting cooler as the sun began to set. Yarin turned and led Jada away from the disturbance. To distract her from her concerns, he pointed out a large flock of birds on the horizon – hundreds and hundreds of them, flying together in formation. Their silhouetted bodies made interesting patterns against the fading light of the day. Their presence here was unusual. Yarin and Jada stood close together, looking up at the sky and watching the spectacular display.

28
"... AT TWILIGHT YOU SHALL EAT MEAT ..."

Thwack!

Something startles me. I realise I've been staring blankly again – not aware of what's happening around me. Not really thinking either – just staring. What time is it? How long has Haki been gone? I have no idea how much time has passed while I sat here staring at nothing.

Thwack!

What was that? It sounded like somebody dropped something heavy, but I can't hear any footsteps or a voice. There's nobody around. They're all off protesting so the camp is deserted. I crawl reluctantly to the entrance of our tent and look around. Everything seems normal at first glance. I don't feel like going out to investigate properly, so I sit in the opening and make myself comfortable there.

The evening sky is a deep purple-red colour. Adalia would love it. Huh – Adalia. Haki is out there now, still searching for her. He thinks I don't know he's been working his sandals off, making enquiries about Adalia every day. Today he said that he was joining the protest, but I don't believe *that* for a second. Yesterday he was "learning about the structure of the tribes". What a terrible liar – he always has been – and he still thinks he can fool his best friend! I'm letting him look for her though.

I know it's a hopeless chase, but at least he's stopped nagging me and I can sit in peace doing nothing. As I sit here, Haki's words return to my mind. They keep haunting me and I wish I could make them go away:

"Who would she have trusted? Who would she have gone with?"

I feel myself glazing over again and I let it happen – I don't care any more.

Thump!

Bump!

Thwack!

Three large, round objects land in quick succession not far clear of our tent. The sudden sound drags me back into reality again. I squint, trying to distinguish what the shapes are. They have disturbed the dust and it hangs in the air, obscuring the objects and blurring my vision. I can't decide what they look like. Instead I look around to find the source. There is no indication of where they might have arrived from. As I am still wondering how that can be, another lands slightly further away. And another to my right. They keep coming and coming.

Thump! Thud! Bump! Thud! Bump! Thump! Thwack!

The drumming resonates all around the camp like giant solid raindrops. I reach out for one of the beached blobs and grab hold of something that feels soft and feathery. I drag it back towards me. As I pull it closer, its shape becomes more familiar. The fat body, the two spindly legs. The beak is small too. It's a quail. A quick look back at the other objects confirms that they are as well. I recognise them much more easily now, despite the increasing amount of dust. Large quails – small quails. Quail meat! And there's *plenty* of it. I get to my feet. I'm eager to get out there before the others get back. I'm going scavenging!

29

"... GATHER A DAY'S PORTION ..."

I watch as the fine white flakes float through my fingers and drop softly back into the bowl. I scoop them out into my palm to enjoy the tickly feeling as they settle on my skin. With my hand carefully positioned over the bowl, I spread my fingers and tip my hand slightly to encourage the flakes into motion. I notice how they twist and turn along the way. Each one is so detailed and delicate. So perfectly formed. They dance together like grains of sand through an hourglass. I repeat this whole process and watch captivated once again, before I go on collecting.

It is my turn to gather the manna today. I must collect enough for Yarin and Jada, as well as for Nati and me. I must collect enough to last us for today *and* tomorrow, because tomorrow is the Sabbath and apparently there will be no manna on the ground. The job must be done every morning after the dew evaporates, but before the sun is hot enough to melt the flakes – and it is a really frustrating job. That is why we are taking turns. It is true that the flakes cover the ground like a blanket. They are literally everywhere so the whole surface appears white. It seems at first to be a simple task to collect them – but it is not really. The flakes of manna are small, fiddly to pick up and easily blown away in any breeze. As well as that, many, many people are out gathering for their households. It is difficult to reserve an area for your work, so already this morning I have bumped into several people as I have scrambled around on my hands and knees and had to move twice to find enough to feed the four of us.

Now I am tired and fed up and the bowl is still only half full. As I continue to crawl around, defending my latest patch as much as possible, I try to make the time pass more quickly. I don't feel like singing so I try something that Jada suggested to me: listing things I am grateful for. I think of Nati and smile. I think of Jada and Yarin and the way they have helped me whenever things have been tough. They have made me feel valued – loved even. Like I imagine my parents would if they were still here. I add Elim to my list, thinking of how much better I felt after resting there. The sunlight, warmth and incredible views along our journey.... The fact that I have stayed safe through all the obstacles.... Water to drink.... And this food too – I look down at the bowl and I am stunned to see that it is nearly full now. I have been so distracted by my thoughts that I have hardly noticed the effort of my work. I can soon return to the others. Suddenly I feel much better about everything. *Clever Jada!* I can't help grinning at her ingenuity.

30

"I MAY TEST THEM, WHETHER OR NOT THEY WILL WALK IN MY INSTRUCTION ..."

"Haki, come out here!"

It is my turn to gather the manna today. I am ready to go collecting. Except there's a small problem. There is no manna. None. I am looking in disbelief at the ground outside our tent, where yesterday and every other day this week there has been a layer of the strange sweet substance. The same ground is now empty. Not a trace of manna can be seen anywhere.

"Haki!" I call more urgently.

Am I too late? Have I missed my chance? The dew is still evaporating from the ground. The sun is not yet hot enough to melt the manna. It should be here. I don't understand. Am I dreaming? I squeeze my earlobe hard between my thumb and forefinger. *Ouch!* No, I'm not asleep. I'm definitely awake. And there's definitely still no manna, no matter how fiercely I glare at the ground. I stare so hard that my vision actually blurs.

"What's the problem?" Haki is emerging from the tent, looking drowsy. I see no point in wasting words when a simple gesture will do the job – and do it just as well. I move my open palm in an arc to indicate the area in front of us.

"No manna?" His eyes look questioningly at me. I confirm his observation.

"No manna."

"What now?"

"I don't know, Haki."

"Maybe we should have collected more yesterday, and saved some. We could have boiled…"

"We tried that the other day," I remind him.

"Yes."

"And that was a total disaster."

"Yes, you're right. It was a total disaster."

"It stank!"

Haki waits a moment, straight-faced, before adding a clever remark: "The worms seemed to enjoy it." I can't help laughing, despite our current predicament, and Haki is soon laughing too. We haven't laughed together like this recently. Not since I gave up on my quest. It feels good. Really good. I should let myself laugh more often. I must stop blaming myself. Feeling much more positive again, I'm the first to compose myself and stop laughing. I echo his earlier question.

"What now?"

Haki stops laughing too. He shrugs. He is looking at me oddly, trying to decide something. When he speaks, he hurries his words.

"I'm off, then."

"Where are you going?" I ask. His reply is a mumble – deliberately too quiet for me to hear – and he is already walking away.

"Haki, wait." He slows, uncertainly.

"I know that you've been looking for Adalia."

I notice Haki's eyes widen involuntarily like a thief caught in the act, before he looks away and gazes down at his feet.

"It's all right." I pause. This is difficult for me to admit. "I don't mind. I'm… " I sigh, trying to find the best way to express myself. "I'm quite grateful actually."

Haki looks relieved.

"I shouldn't have given up. I was frustrated but…"

"Kiva," Haki interrupts. His tone is solemn. "Nobody here has seen her."

"I kept thinking about what you said," I say.

Haki looks puzzled.

"About who she trusted enough to go with. I couldn't think of anyone at first. Not for ages. Then it occurred to me."

"What?" He asks with his brow furrowed in interest. "Who?"

"I know where she is. Let's go."

"Wait. Hang on. Where? Tell me…"

"There's no time. I've wasted far too much already. Come on!"

Adrenaline surges through my body and I feel better than I've felt in days. I'm certain that I've finally solved the puzzle and it feels great. Now all I have to do is get to Adalia, and I'm bursting with anticipation and excitement. I'm already strides ahead of Haki, who seems totally baffled. I laugh. Life is good.

"Come on!"

31

"... GIVE US WATER THAT WE MAY DRINK ..."

My knees feel like they are about to give way and my back is throbbing. Nati is riding on my back, her full weight pressing into my arms. My feet and legs are managing to carry both of us, but only just. It's the end of another long, tiring day's travelling. My pace has slowed, my stride has become a lot shorter.

Occasionally I lose balance and sway to one side or the other. I'm concentrating hard to make sure that I don't trip or stumble. Nati is not asleep, but is unusually quiet and still. Her normal bubbly enthusiasm for life is not here today. She seems distant and gloomy – unlike herself – and I miss her chatter. The lack of conversation has made the hours seem longer.

Usually I would have asked Yarin to take Nati for a while to give me a break, and usually he would have been eager to help me, but not today. Today I didn't even want to ask. Yarin has walked with Jada since sunrise, supporting and encouraging her; sometimes offering her his arm, sometimes holding her hand, sometimes putting an arm around her back. He has not once left Jada's side. I spent a lot of time watching them while I walked. I noticed how frail Jada looks and remember how old I had thought she was when we were neighbours in Goshen... And how young I had felt then. I haven't thought of them as old for ages now. Today though it was plainly obvious to me again. I realised for the first time how difficult all this must have been for Jada. She was forced to leave a well-kept and comfortable home. Though they didn't have much, Jada had always made it homely and welcoming. Her frail, elderly legs have carried her across miles and miles of rough and unfriendly ground. She has coped at times without food, supported me through my crises. And she has smiled through it all. I have been impressed by Jada.

I remember how frustrating I found her to begin with and realise that I have grown to respect and trust her.

I look up and notice that Judah's standard is being hammered into the ground alongside a rock face ahead and I am relieved to be able to rest, but I'm especially grateful for Jada's sake, and for Yarin who has tended to her all day and who looks tired. I mark out an area for us and signal to Yarin to join me. He steers Jada gently in my direction. Nati is curled up amongst our few belongings. She is listless and shows none of her usual enthusiasm to explore. Yarin settles his wife beside her. Jada's frame seems small and she hunches over, her head hanging low. She has lost weight recently and her arms are thin. I don't think that I'd have recognised her if I'd seen her again for the first time now. Though we have only travelled for a few weeks, Goshen is already a distant memory, another lifetime. Jada seems to have aged a decade in that time.

I am totally absorbed in my observations, squeezing one thumbnail between my teeth as I watch. Yarin gently taps on my elbow and startles me. I take a sharp breath in and cast around with a blank expression on my face before my mind catches up and I realise what's happening. Yarin pulls me aside. I tear my eyes away from the two exhausted figures, lower my hand from my mouth and attempt to give him my full attention. Yarin is speaking in an urgent whisper.

"Adalia, there's no water. I overheard some men—"

"Are you sure?" I surprise myself with the calmness of my question.

"Yes." Yarin looks at the ground. It is the first time I have seen him look unsure. I am waiting for him to go on. He doesn't. It seems he is waiting for me.

"Yarin," I am not feeling as confident as I sound, but I wait for him to look up and I meet his gaze. "It will be fine." I repeat my words to emphasise them. "It will be fine."

"I don't know, Adalia. Jada is weak and with no water—"

I cut him off a second time.

"It will be *fine*, Yarin. We have been without water before and God has provided it. He will provide water now."

As I speak, my confidence grows. I do believe what I am telling Yarin. I believe God will provide for his people.

"Go and sit with Jada now. She needs you. Talk to her. Comfort her. Reassure her. I will get everything else organised." He turns to go. "Yarin," I add, "I don't think you should tell her what you have just told me."

He nods his agreement.

I take a deep breath. When did I become the steady, dependable one amongst us? It is not only Jada who has changed, worn down physically by this journey, but Yarin too is different. The constant difficulty has made him doubt. And I hardly recognise myself from the naive girl I was before. A few weeks ago the only responsibility I had was for a few sheep. Now I have a child to think about and the welfare of two elderly friends – a lot for a girl as young as me to manage on my own. I pray a simple request as I work: "Lord, give us water."

My eye is drawn to the ever-dancing scarlet and gold ribbons of fire above us and I know in my heart that he will.

32

"BUT THE PEOPLE THIRSTED THERE FOR WATER ..."

 The more I think about it, the more certain I am that Adalia went to our neighbours, Jada and Yarin, for help. The trouble is that I can't remember which tribe they belong to. I've heard them talk about it before but, the harder I try to remember, the vaguer the conversation becomes in my mind and the less I can rely on the memory. It's so frustrating! I'm annoyed with myself for not paying proper attention to their words. At the time it had seemed dull and unimportant. Now I realise it could have saved me a lot of trouble.

We've already battled our way through Naphtali, and Haki had single-handedly interrogated the people of Asher to confirm Pagiel's words were true. Before leaving what Haki and I like to call the "camp of the falling feast", we'd eliminated the tribe of Dan as a possibility. We'd split up to speak to as many people as possible, tackling one part of the camp each day until there were no family groups left to ask. I'd described Adalia to them and told them it was likely she was travelling with an older couple. Haki had told my story more elaborately, embellishing it with emotion, making people feel sorry for me and Adalia so that they would think harder about what they knew. No one had seen or heard of her though. Just to make sure, Haki and I spoke to the tribe's leaders, but Yarin and Jada were not known in the tribe of Dan. So, as far as we knew now, Adalia was nowhere in the entire camp of Dan. We'd eliminated three tribes. One military group. A quarter of the nation of Israel.

We travelled again and, at the next place Israel stopped, we continued searching in the same way. The camp of Ephraim: the tribes of Benjamin, Manasseh, and Ephraim. I tried to be methodical. Every morning I'd agree with Haki which areas we'd each be searching, and every evening we'd compare notes on our progress. The days passed quickly with much activity and purpose. Once, in Benjamin, a young woman said that she'd seen Adalia. My heart was in my mouth as she led me to the place. I was shaking and felt shivery, and my palms were sweating too. The anticipation was too much to bear so I didn't hear any of what the woman was saying as we negotiated a path through the campsite. As she pointed out the figure, stirring a pot of manna over a small fire, my heart sank and the hopeful anticipation turned to bitter disappointment. I could see immediately that this was not Adalia. I thanked the woman politely but quietly and carried on, though much less enthusiastically after that.

I'd let myself believe for a joyful moment that my search was over and then I'd been let down, once again. The whole task seemed overwhelming to me. Impossible even. All the same, I couldn't let myself give in to doubt again. I'd already lost too much time that way. Eventually, Haki suggested that we move on to the camp of Reuben and I had to concede that we'd done all we could in Ephraim. Neither the ordinary people nor the leaders there had been able to help us in our search.

The same pattern emerged in the camp of Reuben. We searched the tribe of Gad first, then in Simeon and lastly in

Reuben. Again we travelled. Again we camped. There was an occasional false alarm, but mostly we were met with blank faces and shaking heads. I was struck by the willingness of people to listen, but equally by how quickly they were able to forget and go back to their lives.

Of all the hundreds of thousands of people here, only Haki shows genuine and lasting concern. He still searches with me faithfully, day after day. Uncomplaining. Unrelenting.

Today we have reached a new stopping place. They call it Rephidim. I'm grateful because it's much easier to keep track of which people we've already spoken to when they're not moving around.

This morning we agreed to move into the camp of Judah, beginning with the tribe of Zebulun. Haki has gone to the very edge of their campsite one way, where a rock face borders the camp, and I'm starting at the other side of the camp. We're going to work our way through the families here and meet back in the middle this evening.

I approach a small gathering of people. They are smiling and laughing together over a meal. It reminds me of why I want to find Adalia. I want to reunite our family. We belong together, just like these people.

"Excuse me," I say. The father figure stops speaking and seven faces turn towards me all at once. They are a united group. I feel a small pang of jealousy. It isn't the first time I've felt that as I've met families like this one.

"I'm looking for my sister." I begin to describe Adalia to the attentive listeners. The speech is well-rehearsed by now and I recite it almost without thinking. The words pour over my lips almost by themselves. I manage to answer the family's questions easily, without effort. They are the same ones I've answered a thousand times before. "Yes, she resembles me a little. No, she is shorter. Pretty? Yes I suppose…" I break off as a disturbance erupts nearby. A sweating, out-of-breath Haki is tripping over his own feet in his desperate attempt to reach me. He careers into a tent and sends it hurtling to the ground in a mangled mess.

"Kiva! Kiva, I…" He pokes his head out of the fabric, brushes the dust from around his mouth, and pants. He has been running hard.

"Do you have some water?" I ask a woman in the group, who is looking concerned at Haki's dishevelled appearance and horrified at the state of the tent.

"No," she replies. "There is none here." She nods towards Haki, who has collapsed onto the ground. "He shouldn't be running like that in this heat. He'll dry out."

I nod and kneel down in front of Haki, encouraging him to take deep breaths.

"Judah," He puffs. "They're in Judah." I do a double take. My eyes widen and my jaw drops.

"Are you sure? How do you…?"

"I found a young couple who… who know of Yarin… and Jada. The woman has a… has a cousin. She… married their son."

Haki is still gasping heavily between words. I drag him away from the stares of all seven faces. I'm speechless. Thoughts are racing through my brain, but I can't put them into words. Instead I punch Haki's arm triumphantly and grin. Between breaths, he smiles.

"So, are we going?" he asks, pulling himself to his feet. Much as I'm bursting to set off immediately, I pull him back down.

My reply is firm: "Not until we've found you some water."

33

"... YOU SHALL STRIKE THE ROCK ..."

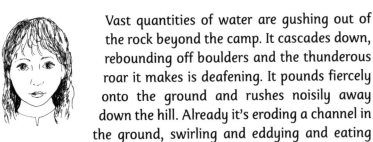

Vast quantities of water are gushing out of the rock beyond the camp. It cascades down, rebounding off boulders and the thunderous roar it makes is deafening. It pounds fiercely onto the ground and rushes noisily away down the hill. Already it's eroding a channel in the ground, swirling and eddying and eating away at the surface. A large crater has formed where the water first makes contact after its rapid descent. A pool, which did not exist yesterday, is now an eye-catching attraction as the sunlight catches on the ripples, shimmering and sparkling. Crowds have gathered to admire the powerful force of the torrent and the astounding beauty of the spray. A fine mist is rising high into the air around the waterfall, moistening and refreshing the whole atmosphere. I breathe in, enjoying the cool sensation. As I watch, light catches the droplets, creating rich jewel-like colours: ruby, emerald, sapphire. A clear double rainbow arcs over the curtain of falling water. I smile. I've been smiling since I first woke up and realised from the sound that God had answered all our prayers. When I got here and actually saw it, my smile grew wider. I feel fantastic. It occurs to me that God is not only quenching our thirst with this waterfall, but also providing a thing of beauty to lift our spirits. I am inspired.

Remembering what I should be doing, I pick up the jug that is lying by my feet and stroll down the hill, following the fast-flowing course of the water. I weave in and out of the crowds who are flocking in the other direction, uphill to see the fall. A short way ahead, I can see a quieter spot where the water meanders and where people are kneeling on the bank to drink. I steer myself towards it, looking forward to the cool, fresh taste of the water and humming happily to myself. I watch people as they rise from the bank, their thirst quenched, and carry their vessels back to their families.

My eyes drift from one contented person to the next until a sight stops me in my tracks. My gaze settles on a figure I recognise. I freeze, questioning what I see. It can't be. I blink and look again, harder this time. *Kiva?* I start to move again. I hurry towards the figure. My vision is focused only on his form. *I thought you were dead.* I speed up, breaking into a run. *Oof!* I bump into someone going the other way. I drop the jug. Hastily, I pick it up, mumbling an apology as fear sweeps over me. *Have I lost him?* I pull myself up. I cast around for the familiar shape. *Kiva? Are you really here? Where are you?* I feel my panic rising. My eyes dart around, trying to find him. My mind can't process the information. *There!* The figure disappears into the crowd. I run again to keep up. *Don't stop, Adalia. You can't lose him now!* People are coming towards me: too many people, passing on either side, filling the scene, blocking the sight of my brother. I weave in and out, stop, stretch up onto tiptoes, crane my neck to see, but Kiva – if it really was Kiva – has gone.

There is no sign of him anywhere. I check again, left to right, right to left, looking further and further into the distance. Eventually I drop back down onto my heels and sigh. My good mood has vanished as quickly as the figure did. I stand staring sadly at the horizon. I automatically turn aside to let people pass. Without thinking, I sidestep back. My body is doing this strange dance by itself. My focus still lingers with the disappearing Kiva-boy. Part of me wants to carry on going and search for the figure until I find him. The more sensible part is thinking of Nati and her hot, clammy forehead, and of Jada whose body is slowly wearing out. It is thinking of Yarin, who I left behind to look after them both. This new grown-up part of me wins the internal battle. I sigh again, turn back towards the water with the jug in my hand and push all thoughts of Kiva out of my mind.

It probably wasn't him anyway. It can't have been. Kiva died in Egypt.

Just forget him, Adalia. Don't think about him any more.

34
"CHOOSE MEN FOR US AND GO OUT."

On the horizon a large army was gathering. Many men were taking their positions alongside one another. One or two particularly solid-looking figures addressed the others, barking out commands, instructing their men on tactics, giving out orders. The army were standing straight and tall, forming a terrifying wall of soldiers. Each man was armed and hostile. Together they were extremely dangerous. Some of the men stamped their feet loudly on the spot in a marching rhythm. Others chanted, growled or spat on the ground like angry camels. From their vantage point, hidden from view, they were watching: they monitored their target and waited for the right moment to move. They were preparing to attack.

A signal was given and the whole army careered into action like a spring that has been released. They approached Israel from behind, spreading themselves out to surround the stragglers at the back of the procession. Their main advantage was surprise. They moved in quickly, wasting no time. Israel didn't see them coming and didn't have time to prepare a proper defence. Many of the weaker, frailer Israelites were the first victims of Amalek's attack. The most vulnerable were targeted by the aggressive opponent and taken out quickly. It was a savage and gruesome assault.

But then Israel mounted a response. They had been surprised by the sudden attack and they were at an immediate disadvantage, but their strength lay in their organisation. Clear lines of communication ran through each military group, and each tribe, to every family in the nation. Instructions were given and word quickly spread through the masses. Each tribe gathered together and equipped its men. Military banners were raised high into the air to lead the soldiers. An army formed and it marched out to meet the enemy. Israel's camp at Rephidim had become a battleground.

PART THREE: BATTLE

35

"WHEN MOSES HELD UP HIS HAND ... ISRAEL PREVAILED ..."

"Shh, it's all right, Nati. I'm here. I've got you now. It's all right." I am pacing with Nati in my arms. She has been woken by a nightmare and can't settle back to sleep. I wipe her hot forehead with a damp cloth and sweep her matted hair off her pale face. She hasn't eaten anything all day. I rock her small body and sing to her. I am worried, but I have nobody to help me. Nati has been feverish since we arrived here. I am doing the best I can for her, but I don't know what to do next.

Jada, who I have been nursing too, is sleeping. I'm relieved. With food, rest and water, her strength has been increasing little by little. Even so, her body is not even close to being strong enough to travel again and the news of the attack came as a massive shock for her. Yarin left this morning to fight for Judah, and for Israel. Jada was traumatised into total silence when he told her. She hasn't spoken a word since he left.

With Yarin gone, I have had to stay much closer to Jada and Nati. I would have been out looking for help by now if the battle hadn't been declared. As it is, I have to stay close to reassure Nati and to do all that I can for Jada. Nati knows something is wrong and she is scared. Because of her nightmares, I have had little time to think about what I saw by the river. But whenever I close my eyes, I see the figure again. He rises from the bank like before. He doesn't disappear into the crowd this time though. Instead he turns and walks towards where I am standing. As he gets close I see that it is Kiva. Kiva smiles and holds out his hand to me. Then the image fades. I don't know what the dream means. I want to believe that Kiva is alive. I think that is why I imagine that I saw him, and why he is in my dream – because I want it to be true. I know that Kiva is gone though. It wasn't really him by the river.

I peer down at Nati. Her eyes are closed. I hesitate. I look at Jada, then back to Nati. They are both sleeping. I seize my opportunity and go in search of help. It feels good. Immediately, I know it was the right thing to do. There's a buzz around the camp. The atmosphere is contagious. I am soon told that the Israelite men are fighting well and that we already have an advantage over Amalek! Jada will be so pleased when I tell her. I ask some women about casualties and hold my breath. Yes, there have been some, but not too many. The injured are being cared for in tents near the river. The dead are being carried away until they can be properly dealt with. I take a deep breath.

"Is Yarin among them?" I ask.

"I haven't heard the name," a woman replies. "That's usually a good sign. Means he's still out there somewhere."

Relief floods through my body and I smile. A few moments pass and the woman is still looking at me in silence. It is making me uncomfortable, so I turn to go.

"Hang on," she says. "What's your name?"

"Adalia," I reply cautiously. "Why?"

"I thought so. You look just like the other one." I am puzzled and a bit afraid, and it must show because the woman explains: "There was a boy looking for you. Older. Says he's your brother. He's come all the way from Asher to find you."

My heart leaps violently into my mouth and there is a lump in my throat. *Kiva! It was you! You're alive after all!* Suddenly my eyes feel a little wet. I realise I am biting my thumbnail again.

"When did you see him," I blurt out. "Where?"

"Oh. I don't know. Yesterday. Or the day before, maybe. He said he'd be near the rock face for a day or two. Who knows though, with the battle and all..."

"Thanks." I stride off with a real sense of urgency.

"Be careful," the woman calls after me.

I am lost in my thoughts, striding purposefully towards... ouch! Something rams hard into my stomach. I'm winded. Before I can uncurl again, two little arms wrap themselves tightly around my legs and a familiar voice demands, "Where were you?"

I haul the child up so I can see her properly. She has some colour in her cheeks again, but she looks cross with me. I realise that in my excitement I forgot to ask anyone for advice about Nati.

"What's happening?" she asks. "Where are you going?"

"Why are you awake?"

I meet her questions with one of my own: "I'm hungry." It is a demand rather than an answer. I smile, pleased to hear that her appetite, and some of her cheeky attitude, has returned. Her temperature is not quite so high now either. *Thank you, Lord.*

"Come with me," I whisper with a wink. "You're going to meet my big brother."

36

"... WHEN HE LET HIS HAND DOWN, AMALEK PREVAILED."

"After three. One, two, three, lift!"

"Careful. Watch out on your left!" I step to the right. A sword slices through the air exactly where my body just was. The Amalekite soldier is already closing on his next target. I tense involuntarily. That was much too close. The blood-spattered legs I'm carrying begin to slip from my grasp. My palms are sweaty with fear and I can't keep my grip any longer. Haki staggers under the extra weight of the man, whose head rests limply on his right shoulder. His arms are looped through the man's sweaty armpits and his knuckles are white as they stubbornly grip hold of the man's shoulders. He braces his knees against the weight. Haki won't let go. He hates everything about the Amalekites' cowardly attack and wants to personally save as many of our men as he can. He won't rest. He can't bear to leave anyone on the ground. I grab for the legs as they hit the ground and cradle one under each arm, taking my share of the weight again.

"Sorry, Haki."

"Let's go. That way."

Neither of us is old enough to fight, but that doesn't stop us being sent out onto the battlefield. We're rounding up the injured Israelites. We're supposed to leave the dead and concentrate on those who can still be saved, but in the midst of the conflict it's often hard to tell. It's noisy and dirty and it takes all of my attention to focus on dodging the sharp blades of the bloodied swords. Haki and I have agreed to grab and run, and leave the decision-making part until we're clear of the danger.

"This one's got a pulse," Haki announces as we haul the mangled soldier to safety. He's young, in his early twenties. We head toward the river where we'll hand him over. I've no idea what his chances of survival are, and no time to find out. By the time they've found his wound, we'll have found and retrieved the next victim of Amalek's vicious attack. There seem to be more victims today than there were yesterday – many, many more. The women's triumphant shouts of encouragement have turned to concerned cries of anguish. Our initial success has not lasted. The Amelekites fought back stronger and harder. I haven't had a break in hours. I'd have stopped for water if it weren't for Haki's heroic determination. Our soldiers do look terrible, and one day I know it'll be me out there, fighting for Israel. My stomach churns at the thought and I feel faint. Slaughtering sheep is one thing. Slaughtering humans is something entirely different.

I survey the scene for our next wounded soldier. I point out one in the distance that still appears to be writhing in agony. He's right in the thick of the action where it's extremely dangerous, but I also know that, if we get to him soon, he may survive his trauma. Haki nods his agreement and calculates the safest route. I follow his lead. We dodge round behind a one-on-one sparring match on the outskirts, then begin to sprint towards our target, keeping low and quiet so that we don't draw unnecessary attention to ourselves. Out of nowhere a soldier appears and grabs hold of my wrist. I pull myself free of his grasp, but my legs have lost momentum and I fall heavily to the ground. Haki doesn't notice. A rough hand clasps firmly over my mouth before I can shout out.

"Shh," says a deep voice. "Don't draw attention to yourself."

A muscular arm around my waist scoops me up as if I weigh no more than a quail feather. My body is hanging in mid-air. I wriggle and squirm, trying to free myself. The arm holds me firmly as I'm carried away. I kick out, my legs flailing. My feet don't make contact. They find only the air. The hand remains over my mouth, though gentler now. Still, I breathe through my nose. I'm afraid. The ground is swimming beneath me, blurry and indistinct. I feel like I'm going to be sick. Unexpectedly, my feet touch the ground again and my mouth is freed. My knees buckle. They hadn't been prepared to take my weight. I take a deep breath and open my mouth to call for help, but the hand lands on my shoulder and spins me around. Beyond him, the battle still rages.

"Pagiel!"

"I need to talk to you. I had to get you out of there. You were endangering yourself."

"I was rescuing a soldier."

"Kiva, listen. They said I'd find you here."

"Who? What are you—"

"Listen." His voice is urgent. "Israel is suffering a humiliating defeat. We are losing soldiers by the minute. Good soldiers. Strong men."

"I know, I've been… Shouldn't you be…"

"Kiva. You are too young to fight. Your *age* is not advanced enough." He pauses, staring me straight in the eye. I don't blink. "*But*, mentally you are tremendously tough." I remember that Haki's still out there – alone. I scour the distant scene over Pagiel's shoulder to locate him. "And physically you have proved yourself more than capable. You have fought against the odds even to be here now."

I'm confused. I'm not sure what Pagiel is saying. I can't see Haki. *Where is he?*

"You are a warrior, Kiva! It's in your spirit. It's who you are."

I cast around again for Haki. *There he is!* He's reached the wounded Israelite, whose writhing is beginning to subside. Time is running out for the soldier. Haki grabs an arm and yanks with all his might. Pagiel is still talking, but I'm no longer concentrating on his words. The body doesn't budge. Haki tries again. Nothing. He takes the other arm now, digs both feet into the ground and leans his entire weight backward. *You've done it! Well done, Haki!* He's moving. I look back to Pagiel.

"Kiva. I can't make the decision for you. I can't force you."

Look around, Haki, keep an eye open for danger. He is struggling now. He has dropped to his knees and is crawling through the mud, dragging the lifeless mass behind him. *Haki! Look out!* An Amalekite has spotted him and is striding in his direction. *Behind you!*

"Will you fight for Israel, Kiva?"

Leave the body. Run!

"I'm asking you to fight alongside me."

"Haki!" I charge across the tragic wasteland, hurdling over bodies and splashing through pools of blood to get to Haki. I'm too late. I'm not even half way there before the Amalekite reaches his goal. He towers over Haki, who is staring helplessly up at him. The sword is raised high above the soldier's head. There's nothing I can do. *No!* It slices fast through the air. Down, down, down. In an inspired move, Haki lets go of the corpse and rolls sideways. Pagiel has reached my side; his sword is poised to protect me. I close my eyes. A blade tears through flesh. A scream pierces the air. Slowly, I open my eyes. Blood is pouring from a long gash in Haki's side. The soldier has moved on. Anger wells up inside me. He's left Haki to bleed to death. Slowly. Agonisingly. Cruelly.

We reach Haki's side and lift his shaking body carefully out of the mud. We walk in solemn silence until we are clear of danger. Tears are forming in my eyes as Haki looks up at me, pleading. Pagiel puts a hand on my shoulder and breaks the charged silence.

"Let's get this boy to a bed and find him some water." He looks at me and speaks softly. "You could help stop all this, Kiva."

37
"BUT MOSES' HANDS WERE HEAVY."

"Not this one!" Nati calls out, sticking her head back out of the tent. Near the rock face we have found row after row of abandoned tents. The men are fighting and the women have moved closer together for security and comfort. I am looking for some sign of Kiva now. I don't know what I'm hoping to find, but maybe there will be something that will help me find him. I join Nati in the tent.

"See," she says. "Two people slept here." Nati bounds out of the tent and immediately skips on to the next. She is thoroughly enjoying this 'naughty' exploration of other people's tents. I am about to follow her, but something stops me. It is not anything that I've seen, just a sense that I have. *Was Kiva here?* I linger a little longer, trying to place the feeling. I look slowly around. There is hardly anything here, just a few holey blankets laid out on either side for sleeping under and some cooking implements gathered in one corner. I notice that the jug is half full of stagnant water and that the bowls have not been washed recently, but that doesn't help. Everybody left here in a hurry. There is not a single obvious clue to tell us whose tent this was.

I think I know though. I step across to where the blankets are and stoop down. I pick one of them up in both hands, rubbing the rough fabric between my thumbs and forefingers. I bring it up close to my face and breathe in deeply, inhaling the familiar scent. *You were here!* This is Kiva's blanket. It smells just like our home in Goshen. So many memories mingle together with this smell. Some of them are fond, some are emotional, but they are all *my* memories. And they are all Kiva's memories too. They are memories that we share. There is nothing here to tell me where Kiva is now though, so I roll up the blanket, tuck it under my arm to encourage me that he's alive and leave the tent. I don't have any idea where to look for him next. None at all. I may have missed my only opportunity.

I walk back with Nati to prepare something for her to eat and to check on Jada. I take the river route so that I can point out the rainbows to Nati and avoid the fighting. I don't want her to see the horrors of battle. At the place where I had seen Kiva, a chain of women and girls are working. One draws the water and places the full jug on the bank; the next picks it up and passes it to another a few steps along the line. The jug goes from hand to hand like this, in rhythmic motion, all the way to a tent where the wounded soldiers are taken. The empty jugs return in the same way to be refilled. As we get closer, I see that one woman is struggling with the effort. She is pregnant, and the combination of the heat and the toil are distressing her.

"Nati, I need to work here for a while."

"Can I help?"

"No. You have been unwell and must rest."

"What are they doing, Adalia?"

"They are taking water to the men who have been injured."

"Why?"

"To wash their wounds. And also for them to drink. They will be tired and thirsty."

"I want to help get the water."

"No, Nati. Take this. Go to Jada. Ask her to tell you how to boil the manna to eat. She must not do *any* of the work, but she can tell you what to do. Then, save a portion for me and share the rest between you. Tell her I will be there when I have done all I can here. She will understand."

I take the place of the pregnant woman in the chain. She is grateful and sits in the shade of a nearby tree, sipping water from a bowl. I have soon fallen in with the rhythm of passing the water and I find that the time is passing quickly. I am able to think, which is good. I have many ideas about how to find Kiva, all of which are either impractical given the circumstances or very unlikely to succeed. I reject every single idea that I have. It feels good to be working towards a solution though, even if I haven't found it yet. I will.

Evening has come by the time I leave my post. I am amazed at how exhausting the work actually was and I trudge back through the camp, rubbing my aching arms. I am even more surprised to find that Nati is sitting outside the tent wrapped up in Kiva's blanket without a fire.

"Why is there no fire, Nati?"

"Jada is sleeping."

"I will light it. Did you have enough to eat?" Nati shakes her head. "You can share mine. I am too tired to eat much anyway. Where did you put it?"

"I didn't boil any. Jada was sleeping and I didn't know what to do." I am horrified that Nati has been sitting here without food and didn't come to tell me.

"Nati! I told you to wake Jada."

"I tried to. She wouldn't wake up."

This shocks me. I'm extremely concerned. Jada has been asleep all night and, as far as we know, all day too. That is not normal. I dive into the tent and kneel down beside Jada.

"Jada. Jada, wake up." There is no response, just a series of slow, shallow breaths. I hold her shoulders and gently shake her.

"Jada, it's Adalia." I blow softly on her face. I squeeze her earlobe and call her name again. Still nothing.

"Nati! Go for help. I need someone who can help me carry Jada. Be quick."

38
"... HIS HANDS WERE STEADY UNTIL THE SUN SET."

I am anxiously looking around for someone who can help. I wave and gesture to try to attract attention. Everyone is much too busy to notice. We have managed to get Jada to the tent where women are taking care of the soldiers. It is the only place I can think of to take her. I desperately hope somebody will be able to help... And help soon. I don't know how long we have got. I instruct Nati to keep holding Jada's hand and talking to her. It is partly to keep Jada conscious, and partly to distract Nati from the nasty gashes, blood and vomit that surround us. I need to get help.

"Help! We need help here. Quickly!"

I've been here a hundred times already today. But this time is different. It's Haki that's in trouble this time... My best friend, Hakizimana. I'm not leaving him.

"This boy needs help!" I call out again. I look around at the chaos here. Bodies lie in every available space. Women are bandaging limbs and washing wounds. Girls bring water, holding it to the lips of soldiers so they can drink. Those that don't survive are unceremoniously thrown out of the tent to create more space for the new arrivals.

Nobody is coming. Nobody has heard me.

"Hold on, Haki," I whisper beneath my breath. I'm willing him not to give up.

"Would someone please help?"

I approach one person after another, but everyone is frantically busy. One woman is replacing a soggy bandage. The blood is flowing fast. I wince. She ties tight layers of fabric on the wound… One, two, three layers.

The next is prising open a deep gash with her thumb and forefinger. It is unbearable, but I can't look away. She uses a damp rag to clean out the mud and grit from the wound. Eventually I spot an older woman who is giving instructions and directing people. She seems to be supervising everything that happens here. I stride towards her.

Pagiel has gone. He's left the troops alone much too long.

A girl is assessing Haki's injuries. She looks worried. That's not a good sign. Water arrives… And bandages. Haki looks pale now. His eyelids are flickering.

"It's going to be fine, Haki." I hold his face in my hands. "Look at me. Stay awake. They're fixing it now." I hope that I sound confident… That he can't see the fear in my eyes.

The girl signals to a supervisor. She's coming over! I'm in the way though. I move away and hover a short way off. I shift my weight from one foot to the other. I can't bear it. It's too much. There's nothing I can do to help. I start to walk. I don't know where I'm going. I just want to take my mind off everything.

The woman has not seen me. She heads away towards another more needy case. I almost collapse in frustration. Jada needs her help. Despite my desperation, I know that these men need her help more urgently. They are in pain. Jada is peaceful. So I wait. I chew on my thumbnail. I tap my foot, nervously, impatient for someone to notice me. I look back at Nati who is faithfully holding onto Jada's hand. *Good girl. Thank you, Nati.* Someone is gently pushing me aside to get past. I turn to find myself looking straight into a pair of very familiar eyes. I gasp.

My mind races with all the events of today. Pagiel wants me to fight. He wants me to help defend Israel. Help prevent scenes like the ones that surround me in this cramped, chaotic space. Haki lies bleeding. He may be dying. There's nothing I can do to make it better. No one seems to want to help me. I look around for someone, anyone. Wait... What's that?

"Yarin!" He is as surprised as I am. "Are you hurt?"

His face and hair are covered with mud. His clothes are torn and ragged. He looks exhausted. But he is standing.

"Hello, Adalia. It's very good to see you."

He smiles warmly and draws me into his arms.

"My leg has been cut. It's not a deep wound, but I am in a lot of pain. It means I can no longer move very quickly. I will not fight again now."

I nod, relieved that the injury is not worse and pleased that Yarin is back with us. I look into his eyes and breathe in deeply, wondering about the best way to break my news. He notices my struggle.

"What is it, Adalia?"

"It's Jada. She did not recover from the news of the attack."

Yarin closes his eyes in grief. His smile fades. He seems sad, but I don't think he is surprised. I lead him to her, slowly because of his limp. Nati greets Yarin with a beaming smile and flings her arms around him. When she finally lets go, I take her hand and lead her away, leaving Yarin to be with his wife.

"Adalia!"

I lose sight of her for a scary moment, but spot her again, holding the hand of a young child. I force my way around the various bodies towards my sister.

"Adalia!"

She looks up, stares wide-eyed and uncomprehending, then darts towards me. We stand facing each other, neither one knowing what to say. Each drinking in the moment. *I've found you.*

"Adalia."

"Kiva. I thought you were…"

"Shh." I put a finger to her lips to stop her. *I'm so sorry you had to go through that.* We hug each other for a long time. "I'm glad you're here."

"Me too," she replies, nodding solemnly. I stand looking at my sister. She stands looking at me. There's so much to say, but I can't think of anything that seems important now. I stand here, letting the tension fall away. The burden of guilt that has gone with me all this time is fading. *Adalia is safe.* I've found her.

 I'm standing face to face with my brother for the first time in weeks. I want to tell him about Jada. I want to tell him about Nati! I want to tell him about the journey and the struggles and about how much I've changed. I want to ask him so many questions, like where he has been and how he got here and why he is so dishevelled but the words stick on the tip of my tongue. *Why are you here? Are you hurt? Surely you haven't been fighting.* I fling my arms around Kiva again and sob. With my head on his shoulder, I let the tears stream down my face. *My brother is here!*

39

"... WITH THE EDGE OF HIS SWORD."

All around me people are celebrating. The battle is over and Israel is victorious. In the midst of the festivities, Pagiel is lowering the standard of Asher. He has asked me to attach the long, silvery ceremonial streamer to the pole, just beneath the banner. It is an honour to be selected from all the warriors of Asher, and I approach the task with great pride. I stand tall and step up to the standard. This ribbon will indicate to any future attackers that we have been victorious once before – that men have been killed with the edge of the sword of Israel. It will also remind us of our success in times of doubt. It marks us out as champions. Each military banner in Israel is being adorned in this way. A unified nation: united in our journey, united in battle, united by our God who guides and protects us.

As I tie the ribbon securely to the pole and watch it rising high into the air once more, I think again of Adalia. I wonder where she is now and what she is doing. Our one and only conversation was extremely limited, cut short by her commitments to Yarin and Jada, and to the beautiful little girl she was taking care of. I was immensely proud of her that day. I saw the confident, caring young person Adalia has become and my heart swelled with pride. I hardly recognised her from the little girl I'd lost in Goshen, but I knew my little sister had blossomed into a beautiful young person.

"Pagiel has asked me to fight alongside him, Adalia."

She had swallowed hard and taken her time before responding. It was painful for her to let me go again so soon.

"Then you must go," she said bravely. The memory of Adalia's courage stayed with me and spurred me on to face each warrior, man to man. It gave me hope.

I didn't want to leave Adalia either. I wanted to find out everything about her journey. But I too had commitments to fulfil. I had to return to Haki and then I had to join Pagiel in battle. I had decided that he was right. I knew that God had watched over me through my whole journey. Now I could see that he had watched over Adalia through hers too. My word to my father was fulfilled. I had kept my promise. I had made sure that Adalia was safe. I know that God will watch over me as I fight for his people and I know that he will watch over Adalia whether or not I am there beside her.

I step back from the standard to see its full effect. The sunlight radiates onto the fabric, giving it an amazing ethereal quality. It seems extraordinary. Set apart.

I linger, letting the image engrave itself on my memory before I turn and walk away. I want to remember it always.

I will go and sit beside Haki for a while now. I will tell him all that has happened today. I don't know if he can hear me or not as he lies there, motionless, but I like to think that he hears and that one day he will open his eyes again. Haki did not leave my side all the way here. I won't leave his now. I'll tell him all about the ceremony, about the altar that our leader Moses built here and that he named it *Jehovah Nissi* – the Lord is my banner. Haki will like that. Sometimes I think he has more faith in my God than I do.

40
"... THE LORD IS MY BANNER."

I stand near the stone altar on the hill. It's beautifully still and quiet here. I wanted to come alone to see *Jehovah Nissi* for the first time, so I waited until everyone else had left. Now I am looking out from this vantage point over the whole of Israel. God has guided this nation, and protected them every step of the way since we left Egypt. I wonder whether everyone in each of the 12 tribes has their own story of God's leadership as remarkable as mine. I suspect that they do. I believe that is why they all came here – to the altar Moses built to *Jehovah Nissi*. The thought is overwhelming.

Jada is gone. Her life has ended now. She did wake up once more, when Yarin was with her, and smiled at him. That is how I found them after I left Kiva. Then her heart stopped beating and her eyes closed, but Yarin still held her hand lovingly in his. I am glad that she saw him. I am glad that he saw her.

Nati wants to find her own family again and she wants me to help her. I'm sad that soon I will have to let her go, but I have enjoyed my 'gift from God'. Nataniella has taught me a lot about myself. I hope I have given her something as valuable as the memories she has given me.

I am grateful too that I know the truth about Kiva. I don't know all the details and maybe I never will, but I do know that Kiva's story did not end in Egypt. I do not have to doubt or question that any more. I know that God will lead him and I know that God will lead me.

I lay down Kiva's blanket next to the altar, then look out again over Israel and wonder where God will take me next. I don't know the answer, but I am not afraid.

Jehovah Nissi: The LORD is my banner.